Also by Kathy L. Salt

I Love You, Nora Whispered

Stargazing

Out of Hand

A Tale of Spiders and Canned Soup

I0543881

A big thank you to my wife, who let me be when I wanted to write twenty-four hours a day, even during our summer vacation. I want to thank Marco, my beta reader, for the immense job he did and all the suggestions he gave that made this book better. I also want to thank my editor, Miranda, whose comments and encouragement made editing easy. Lastly, I want to thank Ava, my friend, who drew the beautiful sparrow that sits on the cover.

Bittersweet
and
Sparrow

Book 1 of the Waerdarei Series

by

Kathy L Salt

2021

Bittersweet and Sparrow © 2021 Kathy L. Salt
Triplicity Publishing, LLC

ISBN-13: 978-1-970042-14-6
ISBN-10: 1-970042-14-1

Printed in the United States of America
First Edition – 2021
Cover Design: Triplicity Publishing, LLC
Interior Design: Triplicity Publishing, LLC
Editor: Miranda Campbell - Triplicity Publishing, LLC

You know who you are. I wrote this one for you.

Chapter One

She had always loved cherries. Bittersweet, ruby red, and so very forbidden. Only the Madams were allowed to eat cherries. Sparrow knew she wasn't a Madam but when she saw the cherries in the kitchen she couldn't help but snatch up a couple anyway, put them in her pocket, and run upstairs.

Hiding in one of her rooms she'd stuff her face with them. She hid the pits in various pots around the House. She didn't need to worry that something would start to grow. Nothing in that House was alive. She couldn't remember ever seeing anything grow in any of the pots.

Sparrow was a streetwalker. Although she didn't prefer that term since she wasn't actually allowed to walk any streets. She was only allowed to be here. In the House. Deep in the heart of Rathmoria City, the capital of Rathmoria Emporie. Her country. For whatever reason Chancellor Rathmore, the ruler of the land, had decided that no prostitutes were allowed to roam freely. They belonged to *Houses*. How many Houses existed in Rathmoria Emporie, she didn't know. She could only ever remember this House.

So in this House she was. Waiting. Or working. Today she was waiting. It was Friday morning. The only day she didn't have to work.

She lie on her back with a cherry in her mouth, sucking the juice out of it as she looked at the various

1

patterns that stains created on the ceiling, the rough woollen sheets making her back itch.

Not that she liked the work, but taking time off was almost worse. When they took breaks they weren't allowed to disturb the people working and since no one was allowed to take days off at the same time, having a day off was lonely. And Sparrow hated being alone. More than she hated working.

There were a lot of cherries downstairs, Sparrow thought to herself. She spat the pit out on the floor and grabbed another one from the pile next to her on the bed. *I could steal more.*

As Sparrow chewed on the last cherry, contemplating the rest of the evening, she heard loud steps outside the door. *Fuck.* She almost choked on the cherry when she scrambled off the bed and dove for the pits. She found four and threw them under her bed. *Where was the last pit?*

The door opened and Sparrow could only stare as Madam Crowder stepped into the room and onto the last missing pit.

"Huh?" With a groan, Madam Crowder leaned down and reached her fat fingers under her shoes.

Sparrow kept silent and stared as her fate was being sealed. Once, Madam Crowder ordered Nanfield to whip the soles of her feet; that was not an experience Sparrow wanted to repeat.

"I'm... sorry." They stared at each other.

Madam Crowder shook her head. "I don't have time for this right now. Get dressed."

"Huh?" Sparrow scrambled to her feet. "What do you mean? It's my day off." *You do not get to decide what I wear on my day off.*

"Yes, yes, I know. You can have tomorrow; now do as I say." When she talked, she showed off her yellow teeth. She'd gotten crimson lipstick on them. It made her face look even more grotesque and when Sparrow stood up and came face to face with her she instinctively took a step back, eager to get out of the splash zone. "We have special guests."

"More than one?" Sparrow swallowed, her throat dry. *Please say that one of the other girls will at least take one of them off my hands.*

"Yes." Madam Crowder shook her head. "There are two of them. They're paying immensely well, and I know I can trust you to take care of them." She sighed. "All the others are already busy."

Sparrow swallowed again, feeling her soul sink to the ground in the cabinet where she locked it away. She nodded.

"Yes Madam Crowder." She was living and breathing and human. She needed to eat. She needed clothes on her back and a roof over her head. "Should I meet them by the bar or do you want to send them to one of the reception rooms?"

"They've requested a girl and a room right away." Madam Crowder didn't turn away as Sparrow went to her closet and chose one of her dresses. "Not that one." Sparrow turned back to look at her. "Take the seaweed colored one. It makes your eyes look lighter."

Sparrow nodded. "Yes, ma'am." *If I do as I'm told and on my best behavior, maybe she'll forget about the cherries.*

"I'll give them another drink and then tell our guests to go to room four." Madam Crowder sighed again, the big hoops in her ears chiming as she moved her head. "I expect

3

you to be there in 20 minutes. Have bath water ready. The guests have traveled far and I think they shall both want a bath." With that she left.

Having put on the dress, Sparrow sat down by her mirror and grabbed her make-up. This was the last action she'd do as herself because when she left the room, she'd leave her true self behind. Her room wasn't much. Wooden walls, dark wooden furniture. The legs of her chair were uneven. Still, it was the only place where she was herself. Her own.

Red lips. Blue eye shadow. She skipped the rouge since it didn't make any difference on her dark skin even though the other workers swore by it. She looked at herself in the mirror and sighed. Madam was right. The green dress did make her eyes shine a bit brighter than usual.

Getting up from her chair, she walked over the rough floorboards wearing her moccasins. She still remembered when she'd first moved to the House and gotten splinters in her bare feet.

She opened the door and pressed the bronze button that locked it behind her. She raised her chin. The least she could do was walk with dignity. She left the corridor where the private lodgings were located.

The landing over the bar was filled with laughter and talk, the air thick with perfume and smoke. Underneath it all, high pitched metallic notes played on the pianolotron. Sometimes Nanfield, the Madam Crowder's right hand, played it too loud causing the customers to complain. Tonight it was just loud enough to fill the atmosphere, tricking everyone into thinking there were more people than there actually were.

Sparrow stopped, put her hands on the railing, and looked down. Her customers were down there somewhere and she wanted to see them. She squinted but it was futile. There was too much smoke from both cigars and incense.

"You're in the way." Without looking back, Sparrow recognized Nanfield's voice.

Even though she wasn't scared of him anymore, his soft voice caused shivers to run down her spine. It was a mystery how someone with a voice of honey could be so cruel.

"I'm going, I'm going." She didn't look back at him but walked with long strides and entered room four. Before the door closed, she pressed the button that made the door shine pink.

The room was already heated and somebody—probably Nanfield—had dragged out two tubs, the bronze reflecting the flames from the fireplace. A big bed stood in the corner, the sheets clean. Sparrow could imagine what they'd feel like against her skin. Silky and sweet smelling. Too bad she'd have to work when on them.

In the past, Sparrow had always started by the bed. Feeling the sheet. Checking the mattress. She would've done anything to get to sleep in one of them, but she was older now.

And there really wasn't any time to spare. Not if she wanted everything to be perfect before the customers arrived. Sparrow walked over to the opposite wall, dragging a hose from behind the stone next to the fireplace. How the engineers managed to make a hose of metal and still bendable was beyond her. She dragged it over to the first tub and let it hang over the edge. She went back to the wall and pulled the wooden lever. The pipes inside the wall groaned and a howl arose to almost unbearable levels as steam moved behind the fireplace. A moment later, hot water filled the first tub.

She looked at it anxiously. Any minute now, the door would open and the guests would enter. Sparrow didn't want the awkwardness of them entering with her bent over the tub, not ready for them. The first tub filled and the water stopped on its own. Thanking the lord for new technology, Sparrow moved the hose from the first tub to the second and hurried to pull the lever again. With the second tub filling, she looked around the room, making sure everything was finished.

She liked room number four. She liked the burgundy walls and how the fireplace created comforting long shadows around the room. She looked at the bed. Should she wait for the guests there? Maybe with her dress off of one shoulder, leaving it bare? Men always liked that.

The door opened just as she moved the hose. The room smelled sweet of soapy water and rose perfume. She sprung from her place behind the fire, put both hands behind her back, and looked down at her feet. *Should I kneel?* She decided against it. How silly she'd look if she knelt while they were already looking at her. There were definitely two sets of boots. Sparrow's heart sank. Having two clients at once was... *don't think about it. If you think about it, you will cry.*

"Good afternoon." She curtsied and dared to look up. Face her enemy and meal ticket.

It was two women. Not that it relieved Sparrow. Life had taught her that women can be just as cruel as men. And these two looked... well, cruel wasn't the right term. They were wearing armor but not of the Chancellor's army. One of them wore a green hood with blonde hair sticking out of it. She had a scar on her cheek that ruined her delicate features. The wrinkles around her eyes made Sparrow think that she was older than she appeared. Her armor looked homemade with a brass breastplate held together by leather bands. Her trousers were of simple leather. A leather band stretched across her chest, holding a large rifle on her back.

The other one had dark short hair and golden skin. Her eyes were fixed on Sparrow with a panicked look. Her armor looked more rundown than the first, the breastplate cracked in the middle. She wore a leather cap with a visor turned up. What that visor might do when turned down, Sparrow could only dream about.

At first, neither of the women spoke. *Should I be the first one to talk?* Sparrow wasn't used to her guests not taking what they wanted right away.

"Now what?" The dark haired girl's voice was sharp in the silence of the room.

The blonde threw her a look. "Now we enjoy the hospitality of this fine establishment." Her voice was rich. "I don't know about you, but it's been days since I enjoyed a proper bath."

The blonde still hadn't looked at Sparrow as she walked up to one of the tubs.

"What about her?" The dark haired woman still fixated on Sparrow.

I'm in here too you know. Sparrow didn't know what to say. *I can hear what you're saying.*

The blonde started to get undressed, her breastplate falling to the floor with a thump. Her skin was milky white and covered in scars. "You can go if you want." It took Sparrow a moment to realize that the blonde was talking to her. "Come on, Isabeau. Get in the other tub. The girl prepared the water for us. And it's perfect."

Isabeau folded her arms over her chest and pursed her lips. "I'd appreciate it if you didn't use my name."

The blonde chuckled. "You."

Sparrow looked up at her. She still hadn't moved from the spot by the fireplace. "Yes, ma'am?" Sparrow asked.

"Does the name Isabeau mean anything to you?"

"No ma'am." Sparrow shook her head.

"Well then." The blonde gave Isabeau a look. "Could you bring me one of the soaps, please?"

Sparrow curtsied, chose between the rose and the lavender and brought the rose soap to the blonde. She kept her gaze down as she got closer and stretched her arm so she could give her the soap without being too close.

"You can go now." *Not even so much as a thank you.* "I'm sure you'd rather be somewhere else and not watching us bathe."

"I am not bathing." Isabeau sat down on the bench in the corner of the room and leaned back. Her eyes were closed. "This is a house of sin and I'm not having any of it."

The others won't believe what a strange afternoon I'm having. Sparrow cleared her throat. "Please, ma'am. I'm supposed to tend to the two of you." *Otherwise Madam Crowder will think I didn't do my duties.* She didn't trust the blonde enough to tell her that. Instead she let her dress fall a bit further down, revealing her cleavage. She bit her lip and let her hair fall forward. She met the blonde's gaze. "I'm sure I can help you with something." The blonde's eyes were icy blue. They looked cold, almost dead, as if there was no one home even though her lips were smiling.

"You can go down to the bar and grab us something to eat."

"Please," Isabeau muttered in the corner.

"That Madam of yours served us drink after drink," the blonde said. "So, if you please." She waved one bubbly hand in Sparrow's direction.

"Yes." *Okay. Alright.* This, Sparrow could do. She'd sneak past the western corridor and use the shortcut through the garden to get to the kitchen. Then she wouldn't need to go through the bar and show everyone that she wasn't entertaining the guests as she should, that they preferred food over her.

When she stepped outside the door, she bit her lips to make them darker and plumper and messed up her hair. Just in case she did meet anyone.

It'd become evening. The lights were low and kerosene candles were lit along the hallway. The floor creaked under her feet even when she tried to step softly. She nodded in greeting at Eloise who was leading a man to room number two. Eloise flashed her a wicked smile and rolled her eyes. The man looked young and inexperienced—Eloise's expertise.

At the end of the corridor, there was a short flight of stairs that led to the kitchen garden. The garden was already encompassed in shadow from the tall walls that encircled it, and the sunset was just out of reach. Dark had gathered in the bushes and the trees casted long shadows. The sky was changing to peach.

The cook always gave her anything she wanted when she told her it was for guests. She asked for bread, cheese, and before stopping herself, she asked for the remainder of Madam Crowder's cherries.

Chapter Two

Life was monotonous in the House. Sparrow could count on two hands how many years she'd been at the House but it didn't mean anything to her. It was just a number. The days bled together. The nights became even worse. Sparrow wasn't one to gossip about the guests, not like some of the others, but even she couldn't help but chime in at times.

It was an hour before opening time, the only time they were ever allowed to socialize. Eloise and Henny sat on the big red pillows on the side, and Sparrow sat on the sofa with Lolly on her side. Dolores, the House's youngest, sat in Sparrow's lap. Sparrow was untangling knots in Dolores's hair.

"Last week I had a guest, well, two guests..." Sparrow lowered her voice just in case Madam Crowder or Nanfield were listening. "...who didn't want me at all."

"Talkers." Eloise nodded. "I've had those. They just want to talk and cry and for me to hold them all night." She pouted and then laughed.

"No." Sparrow shook her head, reminiscing about the strange night. "They didn't want anything to do with me. I got them food while one of them bathed and when I came back, one of them sent me into the corner."

"Did they use the bed?" Dolores asked. "For themselves I mean."

Sparrow almost giggled at the thought of the blonde and Isabeau doing anything romantic together. They were too alike. Too square and too hard. It would be like two mountains trying to—

"They didn't. They sat on the bench eating and drinking wine half the night." She scoffed at the memory. "They didn't get drunk though, and they didn't talk." The few words they'd uttered had been as if between old friends and Sparrow couldn't remember. "They treated me like I wasn't there." And that had been the worst part.

She tugged on Dolores's blonde tresses.

"At least you still got the night off," Dolores said.

"True." Sparrow nodded. She'd definitely had worse over the years. "I should be grateful. It was just strange, that's all."

Madam Crowder entered the room. Sparrow closed her mouth and Dolores sat up.

"Good, you're all here." Nanfield came stalking behind her, his limp worse than ever. When the Madam talked with them, he stayed behind her. "In 30 minutes we're opening the doors. I've had a couple of bookings. Eloise, Henny, Dolores, you're all booked. Feel free to check the roster."

Sparrow felt more than heard Dolores whimper next to her and, as discreetly as possible, enveloped her hand in hers. *Please let it be someone gentle or talkative.* She gave Dolores's hand a little squeeze. Sparrow didn't have much hope. It was always the creeps who wanted the young ones.

"The rest of you walk the floors," Madam Crowder continued. "Like usual."

Sparrow stopped herself from scoffing. Madam Crowder spoke as if there were loads of them but in reality there was just two left. Sparrow and Lolly.

"Now make me money." Madam Crowder rubbed her hands together and the girls got up. Dolores gave Sparrow a weak smile before heading up the stairs.

There had been more of them before. Sparrow had once counted 15 beds in the dormitory. But moving to this House had lowered their numbers drastically. Now only five of them remained. And two were supposed to walk the floors. It was incredibly underwhelming. Luckily they didn't have that many customers anymore. Not since the Chancellor had seized power. Still, Nanfield had tricks to make it seem like there were more girls than in reality. Music, smoke, incense, and some strategically placed shadows could fool most people. Especially with complimentary drinks and cigars.

It was a well rehearsed dance. Sparrow moved to the bar and sipped on some lemon water. For once she let her black hair flow free around her shoulders and she wore a flower crown. A dark red dress hung on her frame and off of her shoulders. Her insides were completely empty, as if she'd shown her soul to the door the moment the House opened for the afternoon.

Lolly turned on the pianolotron and Nanfield opened the doors. Sparrow cleared her throat and lifted her head. The parlour filled up. Some of the men spoke to Madam Crowder or Nanfield right away, only to disappear up the stairs without staying at the bar.

Lolly was pulled into the lap of a tall man wearing a black hat. Sparrow slipped behind the bar, hoping that she'd get to stay there for the rest of night, serving drinks and flashing charming smiles to anyone who asked for them. The smoke was heavier behind the bar and it made her eyes sting and tear up. As the evening went on her vision became less clear.

"Girlie, will you be a dear and give me a beer?"

"I want a whisky."

"Give me a bourbon."

Yes sir. Yes sir. Right away, sir. Sparrow hurried to serve them quickly and efficiently.

"Could you get me a glass of wine?" A familiar voice asked.

The world stopped. The music fell away. It wasn't just that it was a woman's voice. No, often there were women in the House. It was that Sparrow recognized the voice.

She squinted, willing her eyes to focus through the smoke. Her hood was black this time but blonde hair stuck out of it. It looked deliberate. As if this woman, whoever she was, took great care in the way she looked.

"Now." She snapped her fingers. "A glass of wine. This is still an establishment, yes? Or has it changed since last week?"

"Yes, of course. I mean, no." Sparrow grabbed a glass from under the cabinet and one of the bottles from the fridge. Her fingers shook as she pulled the cork free and poured the woman a glass. "By yourself today, ma'am?"

The blonde looked at her with a side of her mouth raised. Sparrow didn't like to be scrutinized.

"You're that little thing who tended to me last time I was here." She said. "What was your name again?"

"I didn't say my name," Sparrow said. "You didn't ask for it."

"No, I guess I didn't." The woman brought the glass to her lips. "Do we have access to the same room?"

The bottle started slipping through Sparrow's fingers and she caught it at the last moment.

"Yes, of course ma'am."

"Then bring the bottle." The woman stood up and lifted her glass. "Let's go upstairs."

"What?" Sparrow's heart leapt. "Now? You want to?"

"Am I in the wrong establishment?" Her voice was low. Almost dangerous sounding. Most of their clients usually seemed a bit thick. This woman was something else.

"No, no, of course not." Sparrow wiped the sweat from her hands onto her skirt and took the bottle again. "Please, come this way."

Room four was already occupied so Sparrow took her to room three. If her guest wanted to take a bath, she would need to send for a tub. Otherwise it had all the amenities. They went inside and Sparrow locked the door behind them. The lamp was out of kerosene but the fireplace was lit and provided enough light to light up the bed, the loveseat, and the window. The floor groaned under their steps. *This House is holding on by a thread.*

The blonde walked inside the room like she owned the place. She reached for something inside her armor and pulled out a coin purse which she threw on the loveseat.

Sparrow looked at it for a moment. She didn't want to be at the mercy of this strange and seemingly cruel woman. She reached up and undid the clasps that held up her dress. The blonde looked at her and shook her head.

"There's no need for that," she said. "Leave your clothes on."

"But…" Sparrow looked at the coin purse.

"See it as payment to sleep in your bed." The blonde walked over to the bed and undid her breastplate. "I've got a long day and I'm going to have an even longer one tomorrow."

"There are hotels." Sparrow stood as if nailed to the ground. She couldn't stop looking at the coin purse, her fingers itching to count the coins. "And inns."

"Yes. Yes." The blonde yawned. She'd already lay down on the bed with her head on the pillow. "There are places more suitable for sleeping but there are no hotels where they don't check for your identification." Her eyes closed.

How did she fall asleep so quickly? Sparrow counted silently to 20. Still no movement from the woman on the bed. She looked at the purse again and pounced on it. As silently as she could, she poured it out on the loveseat. It had been a while since she'd seen real money. Most of the clients paid by credits or favors to the Madams.

She counted them quickly. Then she counted again. After that she simply touched them. There was more than enough here. Enough to buy herself free. She looked at the figure on the bed. Who was this woman who'd throw money away like that? She could've given a quarter of it and Sparrow would've been just as happy.

Whoever she was, she was sleeping properly now. Sparrow sighed and refastened the dress clasps properly so they wouldn't fall down. At least she was up here, in a room. No one would question if she didn't go down to the bar again tonight.

She put all the coins back into the purse and then placed the purse out of sight under the loveseat. She got up and tended to the fire. *I need to tell Nanfield to put more kerosene in the lamp.* She went back to the loveseat, lay down on it, and pulled her feet up. She kept her face turned towards the bed. She wasn't planning to sleep. She was going to watch the woman all night.

Sparrow failed. The next time she opened her eyes, the fire had burned down to an ember. Through the curtains, pale dawn shone through. The blonde was still lying on the bed, but she wasn't asleep anymore. She was staring at the ceiling. A candle was lit next to her and the candle light reflected in her eyes.

"Do you want to talk?" Sparrow didn't know where the question came from.

On the bed, without her armor, the woman looked so much smaller. Almost vulnerable.

"I'm not about to blabber my secrets to a whore." There was no contempt in her voice but the statement still hurt. She was still looking up at the ceiling.

Sparrow was getting really tired of being treated like she was nothing. "Don't blabber your secrets then." Sparrow sat down. Her back ached from sleeping on that stupid, curved love seat. "Tell me something mundane."

The blonde made a noise between a chuckle and a sigh. "Why don't you start then?"

"Okay." Sparrow thought for a moment. "I really like fruit. But Madam Crowder never lets us have any. Just some drops of lemon in our water to prevent scurvy."

"You brought us cherries last time I was here." The blonde looked at her then. Sparrow wished they were closer so she could see the blue fire in her eyes more clearly.

"Yes." Sparrow smiled at the memory. "But they weren't for you. I…" She closed her lips. Maybe she was about to reveal too much. She didn't know this blonde. *Better not admit a crime to a person you don't know.* What if the blonde was a police or something? Although Sparrow doubted it. "My name is Sparrow," she said instead. "That's mundane information."

"Sparrow?" The blonde made that noise again. Like a short, mocking laugh. "Mundane indeed."

"Why don't you give me your name?"

The blonde looked up at the ceiling again. "This game bores me now."

"So you're someone important then." *What are you doing?* Sparrow thought. Maybe the sleep deprivation was getting to her. Or the smoke from the bar earlier.

The blonde just shook her head. "I'm going back to sleep now. I suggest you do the same." She closed her eyes but Sparrow knew she wasn't sleeping.

Chapter Three

This time it only took the blonde two more days to return. Before any of the other clients snatched her up, Sparrow found her sitting in one of the chairs, looking at Eloise onstage singing a song very out of tune in time with the pianolotron. Together they made a screeching noise that not even a mother could love. Sparrow grinned at it. At least the noise was driving away most the clientele.

"Same room as last time?" The blonde said when Sparrow came closer.

"Same as the first time," Sparrow said. "Room number four."

"Ask them to send up a tub, would you?" The blonde got up from her chair. "I'm in need of a bath. And food."

Sparrow nodded. She held out her hand to the stairs and let the blonde go first. She still walked with dignity but there was a stiffness in her step that hadn't been there before.

"Nanfield!" She had never dared to call on him that way before but the blonde's presence made her braver. "Can I get a tub to room four?"

Nanfield muttered something from his seat in the corner. He seemingly enjoyed Eloise's singing.

Sparrow and the blonde entered room number four. "Please, get comfortable." Sparrow made a gesture towards the bench. "Nanfield shall be here with a tub shortly and the hot water only takes a minute thanks to new technology."

The blonde sat down on the bench with the slightest hint of a grimace. *Was she hurt?*

Within minutes Nanfield came in with the tub and as soon as he left, Sparrow hurried to fill it.

"Thanks," the blonde muttered as she got up from the bench and walked over to the steaming tub. "Feel free to fill it with lavender this time."

Sparrow was so surprised over the word 'thanks' that she didn't remember to say 'you're welcome.' Instead she went to get the lavender soap. When she turned around again, her grip on the bottle tightened.

The breastplate was gone and her white shirt was off. The blonde was working on her trousers now, wearing only a tank top that ended just above her belly button. Her skin was blue and yellow and a fresh cut branded her left arm. Sparrow swallowed.

"The soap is going to sting," she said in a small voice.

The blonde threw her a look before kicking off her trousers. "Am I paying you to look?" She sighed.

"Wouldn't you prefer it without soap then?" Sparrow insisted. She took a step forward.

"Just pour the fucking soap, alright?"

Sparrow kept her gaze down as the blonde shed the last items of clothing. Sparrow managed to pour a dollop of the sweet smelling liquid into the bath before the blonde got in. As soon as the water hit the cut on her arm—and any other that she had—the blonde sucked in a breath.

"Told you," Sparrow uttered so low that she hoped the blonde didn't hear.

"Oh shush." The blonde leaned back in the tub and closed her eyes. "It's worth it. The hot water. I needed it."

Sparrow took a moment to look at her. The blonde's face looked different now. Tired. Less regal. She had a strong jaw and thick eyebrows. She looked feminine with her blonde hair curling as it got wet. Gentler. Sparrow knew though that soon those eyes would open and whatever soft features her face had would be gone.

"I thought I asked for food," the blonde said without opening her eyes.

"Of course, ma'am." Without waiting any longer, Sparrow put down the soap and headed out the door.

*

An hour must've passed, maybe two. Sparrow stood in the corner, looking through the window at the garden while the blonde sat by the table with a spread in front of her. The blonde had only put on the tank top and the leather trousers. She was sitting on the bench with one of her feet up on the table. Sparrow could see her very clearly through the reflection in the window.

"Why don't you have one?"

"Huh?" Sparrow turned around.

The blonde was holding an apple. She threw it and Sparrow caught it.

It was red and felt surprisingly heavy in her hands. She ran her thumb over the glossy exterior. An apple. She didn't know if she'd ever eaten one in her entire life.

"Thank you." She bit into it with her front teeth and her mouth was filled with a taste of summer. "Oh."

The blonde snorted. "You really don't get much fruit, do you?"

"No I don't." Sparrow swallowed. "We don't really get much variety. The Madams fill us up on cheap food.

Oats. Beans." She took another bite of the apple and chewed it carefully. The second bite tasted even better. "We haven't actually gotten beans in a year or so though, so we have oats, sometimes rice syrup on it if we're lucky."

She expected pity in the blonde's eyes but there was no emotion in those icy depths.

"You don't need to stand over there." The blonde moved to the side and put her foot down. "Sit, I don't bite."

Sparrow approached the table tentatively and sat down on the edge of the bench. Close enough to smell the soap on the blonde's skin and hair. *I need to ask Madam Crowder if I can buy some lavender soap for myself.* Sparrow wanted to smell it again. She finished her apple and threw the core into the fire.

"Good idea." The blonde laughed and threw the rest of her sandwich in the fire.

It hurt Sparrow that the woman would waste food like that, but she looked so amused Sparrow didn't have the heart to begrudge her of that joy.

"What did you do with the money I gave you?" The blonde leaned back and took the cup of ale from the table. She put one arm up and leaned her head against it. "I almost thought you would've skipped town. I'm sure there was enough in there to buy your freedom."

"There was." Sparrow looked down. Would the blonde be angry? Disappointed?

"But?"

Sparrow bit her lip. "I gave it to Dolores." She cleared her throat. "One of the girls. She's just 14. She needed to get out."

When the blonde still hadn't said anything, Sparrow looked up. The woman almost looked impressed.

"What did your Madam say?" Something lit in the blonde woman's eyes. "Did you make her furious?"

Laughter bubbled in Sparrow's chest. "I don't think she knows it was me," Sparrow said. She moved a bit further in on the bench, got a little bit more comfortable. "But yes, she was and is furious." She chuckled. "That's why Eloise is singing. It used to be Dolores. Her voice was beautiful."

"I'm impressed you gave away your freedom like that."

Sparrow shrugged. It had been the right choice. She couldn't have imagined buying her way out and leaving little Dolores in that place. To be eaten alive by...

"My name is Astrid."

Chapter Four

It was getting colder. Sparrow didn't feel it in her skin but she could see it in the frost on the windows and how the pannikin filled with coffee-replacement felt warmer than usual, the heat making her palms itch. She and the girls sat on the bench outside Madam Crowder's room. One by one they were called in to get their annual checkup by the only doctor that was kind enough to come to the House.

Sparrow sat on the far end of the bench, knowing she'd be called last and okay with it. The longer she got to sit here, the less time she'd spend in the laundry room or in the kitchen cleaning and preparing. It was almost like a holiday for the girls in the House. Sure they had to clean and tidy and organize and get prodded by a doctor, but it meant no customers and they'd get coffee-replacement. Nanfield always gave them as much coffee-replacement as they wanted when it was doctor day.

"Your turn," Juliana—Dolores's replacement—said when she walked past Sparrow. Her nose was raised high in the air, as if she had something to be proud of.

Sparrow ignored her. She wasn't there to make friends, or enemies, and if the new girl wanted to be queen, Sparrow would let her. She left the pannikin on the bench next to her and went into Madam Crowder's office.

It was like stepping into another world. The rest of the house was in desperate need of upkeep with chunky flakes of color peeling from the walls. But not in Madam Crowder's room, oh no.

The doctor had pushed the black oak desk back and filled it with his tools. A black tarp covered Madam Crowder's luxurious bed. The carpet was rolled up and stood in the corner. Sparrow had seen that carpet once and knew how soft and lush it felt on her bare feet. The floor didn't need a carpet though; the wood was polished and proper. There was also a working steam heater instead of fireplaces like in the other rooms.

"You're Sparrow, yes?" The doctor looked at her, the majority of his face covered by a brass mask. A spectacle hung over his left eye and there was a meter on his forehead. What it measured, Sparrow didn't know.

"You're not the regular doctor," she said. Their usual one was older and heavier.

"No, I know." The doctor made a gesture towards the screen. "Please take off your clothes and come and lie down on the bed." Sparrow went behind the screen. She pulled off her clothing items one by one and hung them on the iron valet stand. When she was wearing nothing but underwear and stockings she walked out from behind the screen.

"Ah yes." In spite of the mask, Sparrow knew that the doctor was blushing. He turned around sharply and stood by the bed, waiting for her to lie down. "Doctor Kogun apologizes for not being here. He always liked coming here and wishes all you ladies the best."

Sparrow nodded and lay down. The doctor leaned over her. *I hope he doesn't take advantage of his, or rather, my position.*

"I'm going to palpate your…" He cleared his throat. "Body." He took his gloves off, revealing two small, almost feminine hands. They were shaking.

"Of course." Sparrow closed her eyes as the doctor started touching her. He kneaded and prodded her throat, her chest, her breasts, down her sides, and her stomach. He left her private parts alone as he went down one leg, then the other. He was looking for inflammation, abscesses, or other irregularities. Sparrow knew this since Dr. Kogun always explained what he was doing as he was doing it. This doctor kept quiet and breathed increasingly hard.

"Okay." He sounded breathless. "That's done. I'm going to run a blood panel like usual. Are you feeling okay otherwise? No health problems? Getting your..." The skin visible outside the mask was becoming bright red. "Menses as you should?"

How old is this kid? Sparrow didn't know whether to laugh or cry.

"Yes," she said. "I feel just fine." She groaned when the doctor stuck a needle in her without warning first. "Hey!"

"Sorry," he said. "I just wanted to get this part over with."

"You should still give me a warning." Sparrow forced her body to lie still. Her arm started to ache. "What if I had twitched or something?"

"That's what the woman before you said too," he muttered to himself before pulling out the needle. "There, all done."

"How old are you?" Sparrow sat up, resisting the urge to itch her arm.

"I'm 16." The doctor looked down. "But I know what I'm doing, honestly."

"16!?" Sparrow jumped off the bed, went over to the doctor, and took the bandaid that he was holding. She put it where the needle had been instead of waiting for him. "Are

25

you even licensed? Does Madam Crowder know a little boy is here and—"

"I'm not a little boy!" The doctor stood up. He sounded upset. "And I have a license. I started early and it's not like there are any other doctors available."

"No other doctors available?" Sparrow refused to believe this. "Where *is* Doctor Kogun?" She took her hands and covered up her breasts. She started to feel unsure that this wasn't some kind of ruse or joke. Maybe this young boy just wanted to visit the House but didn't have enough funds or…

"He is at war! Okay?" The doctor yelled. "And if you think I'm just going to let you offend me, I…"

"War?" Sparrow moved her head back. "What war?"

"You don't know?" The doctor seemed as surprised as her. "There's a civil war going on, the T.A.L.W. attacked a shipment coming into the capital last night. A shipment of food and medicine, things that the families of the capital need. The Chancellor has demanded that every T.A.L.W. be sentenced to death. Anybody capable is fighting and anybody who's already passed their second year was allowed to graduate early. Doctor Kogun has been sent to the front line and I got to take his place."

Sparrow sank down on the bed. "A civil war?" She hadn't been outside the house in almost 15 years. She couldn't imagine what it looked like. She'd always felt trapped but she'd never felt so cut off from society before. Cut off from the rest of the world. "For how long? The T.A.L.W?" Sparrow had never heard this before.

"For five years," the doctor said. He adjusted his visor. "Well, it's not really as dramatic as it seems. This is the capital. The Chancellor says that the rebellion will not break down our walls." He stood up and went to the window and lifted the curtains slightly so he could look out. Sparrow wanted to join him but the window faced away from the building, not towards the garden, and she wasn't allowed. "But outside Rathmoria City the fight rages on." He took a deep breath. "I think we're done here."

"Yes."

Sparrow watched him pull the curtains back. She turned around and went behind the screen. Her clothes were still there, hanging on the valet. She got dressed quickly.

"I'll send the results of your blood test to your Madam."

"Mmm." Sparrow didn't have anything else to say. As soon as she got dressed, she left the room without saying goodbye.

Nanfield was lurking just behind the door. "Everything went alright with the doctor?" He glanced down at her body, just long enough to make her inwardly squirm.

"Yes." She turned away from him and headed down the stairs. "I shall join the others in the kitchen now." She wasn't going to stay long enough to give him a chance to touch her with his grubby hands.

Of course there isn't a war, she told herself as she walked down step after step. *There are always groups causing problems. Maybe the boy has a romantic view of rebellion and that's why he painted the problem bigger than it is?* Sparrow was eager to believe that there was a revolution going on but she had to admit that the prospects were terrifying, too. If rebel fighters kicked down the door, she didn't know what would happen. She was employed by the state, technically. If there really was a war, what side was she on?

Chapter Five

A new existence had begun for Sparrow. Even though she was worried about the supposed war, she had other things to keep her occupied. Astrid, the mysterious blonde woman, came at least once a week after that. Sometimes for a bath, sometimes to sleep. They didn't talk much. Still, those nights with Astrid were nights that Sparrow longed for. Better than her days off. It made her life less monotone.

That night they were in room number one. Sparrow had fallen asleep on the bench near the fireplace. Astrid was sleeping in the bed like usual. Just like other times, Sparrow woke in the early hours in the morning. She sat up and stretched her back.

She glanced at the figure sleeping on the bed. Sparrow would've given anything to sleep on the empty space next to Astrid but Sparrow didn't even suggest it. There was an invisible line between them that Sparrow respected. *She* would not be the first to cross it. Next to the bed, Astrid's rifle and breastplate leaned against the wall. The flames reflected in the bronze of the weapon and it shone like jewelry. Sparrow had never seen such a beautiful rifle before.

I'm sure there's no harm in just looking at it. Sparrow slid off the bench and crawled closer to the bed. The breastplate looked nice, too. She'd never been close enough to look at the carvings. She thought that it was just scratched from battle or something but when she got closer it looked deliberate.

She turned her head to look at the weapon. Almost everyone out there owned a firearm, Sparrow knew that. She'd probably been taught to fire one as a child. But that was in another life, one she couldn't quite remember. The stock was bronze and there was an inscription on it. Sparrow squinted and leaned even closer.

To arms, liberate Waerdarei.

Under the words was a line that stretched across just above the trigger and twisted into a small bird. *A sparrow.* Sparrow chuckled. *How fitting.* She reached up and touched her finger to the flapping wings of the bird. *But what is Waerdarei?* Sparrow wanted to remember hearing that word somewhere else in another time.

Astrid muttered in her sleep. The sound startled Sparrow and she pulled her hand back too fast. The weapon fell on the breastplate with a thud and both of them fell to the floor. *Oh no.* Sparrow scrambled to her feet and backed away from the bed but it was too late. Astrid sat up and looked to the side. Their eyes met. Sparrow opened her mouth but before any sound came out, Astrid sprung from the bed, walked her up to the wall, and pressed her against it.

Sparrow's heart pounded and she struggled to get free. Astrid pressed her forearm across her shoulders and towered over her.

"What were you doing?" Her voice was low. Calm. Not like she had someone else pressed up against the wall.

"I'm sorry," Sparrow croaked. "I… just… wanted to…" She pushed against Astrid's arm that was getting closer to her neck. "Please, I can't breathe."

"Fine," Astrid pursed her lips and put her arm a bit lower. "Now, what were you doing?"

"I was just looking at it!" Sparrow yelled. "I just wanted to see it." Her mouth closed.

Astrid scrutinized her and Sparrow squirmed but Astrid held her in a death grip.

"Were you told to shoot me?"

What?

"Of course not!" Sparrow was starting to feel light headed. Adrenaline pumped through her veins and she kicked out with her legs. "I don't even know who you are!" She looked into Astrid's eyes. "Please, please, let me go!"

Astrid's grip tightened and a dangerous blue fire swirled in her eyes. She didn't say anything, just kept looking. The silence was scarier than anything. Sparrow swallowed. It felt like Astrid was reading her like a book. Sparrow wanted to lower her gaze but found herself unable to do so.

"You're hurting me," she pleaded. "I don't know who you are. I haven't told anyone. I don't know who you are!"

Astrid took a deep breath. She nodded and finally, *finally,* let go. Sparrow fell to the floor. Astrid looked down for a moment then extended her hand down. Sparrow took it and let Astrid pull her up.

"Don't touch my weapon again."

Was that it? Sparrow felt a twinge of anger as Astrid walked to the bed and lay back down. Just like that.

"You're not even going to apologize?" The words were out before she knew what was happening.

"What?" Astrid turned towards her. There was a hint of an amused smile on her face. "You were the one who touched my weapon. You don't think I'd defend…"

"Defend?" Sparrow took a step forward. "Defend yourself? Against me?" She pounded her own chest once. "Have you seen you? It's me who needs defending against you." She crossed her arms over her chest, her nostrils flaring.

Sparrow wasn't used to feeling anything; it was easier that way. But now anger made her face burn and her skin itch. Anger about everything washed over her. She was stuck here. She was stuck in this House with Madam Crowder. With Nanfield. With the stupid girls who were just as stuck as her. Stuck with clients who used her and hurt her. And stuck with this Astrid who had hurt her and then claimed that...that.... Sparrow lowered her head. *Don't cry. Don't cry. Don't cry.*

"Oh please don't cry." Astrid hit her head on the pillow. "I so don't have energy for this."

"I'm trying not to, okay?" Sparrow leaned her face towards the ceiling and blinked. She took a couple of deep breaths. "It's your fault for scaring me."

"I'm sorry."

Sparrow looked back down. Astrid had sat back up and leaned her back against the headboard. The look on her face was genuine. Sparrow didn't trust it.

"I was startled when I woke up." Astrid sighed. "My weapon and..." She made a dismissive gesture with her hand. "I reacted out of self preservation. I didn't mean to scare you. Well, I did but that was only because I thought you were trying to scare me." When Sparrow still hadn't answered, Astrid patted the bed. "Come on, sit down."

Sparrow walked soft-footed over to the bed and sat down on the edge of it. She sighed when her body hit the mattress. It was just as comfortable as always.

"That love seat is terrible to sleep on," Astrid said. "I don't know how you do it."

"You should see my own bed." Sparrow took the duvet between her fingers, just to feel it. "It's almost just as bad."

"You mean you don't get to sleep in these rooms?"

Sparrow shook her head. "And neither would I want to. I mean, we work here. I don't have that many fond memories of…" Sparrow was saying too much and she knew it. "I just mean, we work here. It's nice to have your own room where you can be yourself."

"I can sympathize with that." Astrid nodded. "Well, it's almost morning but if you want to sleep here for the rest of the night, I'm fine with that. I'll sleep on this side and you can sleep here." She patted the bed.

"Are you just doing this because you scared and hurt me?" Sparrow didn't lie down. She couldn't, could she?

"Does it matter?" Astrid lay down and turned her back to Sparrow. Within minutes she was breathing evenly.

Sparrow looked back at her. *Maybe Astrid is famous for being the fastest and best at falling asleep.* Sparrow snorted. She didn't know how to feel. The anger was still there but less directed at Astrid and more directed at everything else. It was as if being near Astrid made her feel things.

Maybe it would be okay. Maybe nothing bad would happen if Sparrow lay down next to her. Maybe if she just lay down without sleeping. Sparrow rested her head on the pillow. *Oh maker.* She couldn't remember the last time she had been so comfortable.

"Can I ask one thing?" She fought against the imminent sleep.

"What?" Astrid sounded tired as well.

"What's Waerdarei?"

Astrid produced a sound somewhere between a snort and a sigh.

"Well if you have to ask me that, I can't answer. Not right now at least." Astrid sighed again. "The word is in your blood, Sparrow. Think about it. You must remember."

The answer puzzled Sparrow even more.

*

"Hey." A hand shook Sparrow's shoulder, shaking her lightly.

What? Sparrow opened her eyes. Morning light shone through the thin curtains and far away morning bells were ringing. She sat up and rubbed her eyes. "What happened?"

Astrid's chuckle reminded her of who she was with. Sparrow opened her eyes properly and squinted at her.

"You fell asleep, that's what happened." Astrid had gotten dressed, breast plate and all. The rifle was again attached to her back.

Sparrow didn't want Astrid to leave. She was surprised to find that she would've done almost anything to make her stay.

"I wish I could let you keep sleeping," Astrid said. "But I think you'd get in trouble if I just left you here."

"Thanks." Sparrow rolled her shoulders and stretched her arms. Her body complained when she put her feet to the side of the bed. She would've given almost anything to sleep another hour or two.

"Oh, don't say thanks to me," Astrid said. She got up and walked over to the window. She was wearing gloves now too. Thick gloves. She looked like she was going into battle.

Sparrow forced herself up and moved her head from side to side. "Do you want food?" Maybe Astrid was hungry. Maybe Sparrow could get her to stay just a little while longer.

Astrid looked at her with a small smile on her lips. She shook her head. "No, thank you. I really should be going." She walked over to Sparrow. "Do you often tend to female customers?"

"Um," Sparrow blinked her eyes a couple of times. Was she still dreaming? "Yes."

Astrid nodded. "Fair enough." She turned her head to the side. "Do you prefer female customers?"

Sparrow made a sharp intake of breath. It was too early for this. "No one has ever asked me that," she whispered. Her throat was dry. "I think…"

Whatever words she'd planned to utter were stifled in her mouth when Astrid moved slowly, yet firmly closer. Sparrow stood as if frozen to the ground. She held her breath as Astrid's lips touched hers in a chaste and oh so short kiss. Before Sparrow could register what had happened, Astrid pulled back and left the room.

Chapter Six

The House was quiet. Nanfield had hung the *closed* sign on the door and most of the inhabitants of the House had gone to bed. Sparrow was lying in her bed, listening to the silence and occasional scurry of a rat inside the walls. She'd gone up a couple of times to look outside the window but it was still the same, stupid view of the empty kitchen garden. It gave her nothing. The House hadn't had a customer for two days.

If this continues, Sparrow thought, *Madam Crowder will have to sell this House too and we'll have to move into an even smaller one.* She didn't want to think about what would happen then. Maybe she'd lose her job and be sent on to another type of work. She was the eldest in the House now. She knew that Madam Crowder wouldn't want to keep her forever. Sparrow wasn't sure on the actual number, but she could see in the faces of the other girls. They were younger. Their eyes didn't quite hold the amount of despair hers did.

She sat up on the bed and dangled her feet over the side. Her sheet hadn't been changed in months and it felt itchy and dirty on her skin. Not even putting on one of the dresses felt better. She perked her ears for a moment. No, everything was still silent.

What other work was there? Sparrow wasn't entirely sure. Hadn't her mother and father been farmers? She wrinkled her eyebrows, trying to remember. No memories surfaced. Maybe she should just ask Madam

35

Crowder what would happen if they sold the House so she could mentally prepare.

"Let's do this," she whispered. She got up from the bed and tiptoed to the door.

The House hadn't had a customer for two days, three including last night. Surely, there was no harm in having one little nap in one of the nicer, cleaner, beds? She tiptoed down the dark hallway, mindfully avoiding the floor boards that creaked.

She stopped for a moment. Something was very, very off. She turned around and edged back the way she'd come. She went past her own room and continued to Madam Crowder's quarters. Without thinking, she pushed her ear against the wall. *Silence.* Her eyes widened and her heart started pounding. She couldn't hear any of the usual sounds of snoring or muttering that Madam Crowder always gave off when sleeping. Either she was awake or Madam Crowder was not there.

Sparrow leaned down and looked through the keyhole. She couldn't see much but the room was dark without a hint of movement.

Where is Madam Crowder? Sparrow felt like a sheep that had lost its shepherd. She turned around and forgot the tiptoeing. She ran down the stairs hoping to see Madam Crowder, or Nanfield, or *anyone.* The moment she reached the fourth step, a strange whistling sound made her look back. A moment later, something hit the house from above and the upper floor exploded in a hurricane of wood and metal. Sparrow flew forward and landed at the end of the stairs.

When she came to, she turned around. A shriek got stuck in her throat. The upper floor was no longer there. Fire lapped what was left, reaching up into the night sky.

Sparrow's heart was beating its way out of her chest and she felt like she was going to throw up. The flames were coming closer, making their way down the stairs. Sparrow had to get out. Now.

She scrambled to her feet, barely registering that her shoulder was pounding and that one of her feet felt wet. *Get out, get out, get out, get out.* The thought that Sparrow would've been dead if the bomb had dropped just a few seconds earlier was harrowing. It had come from above. Dropped from a plane? It felt as if Sparrow's heart stopped beating. Her brain stopped thinking. She removed all thoughts, all emotions from her head and body. She just needed to survive this.

She opened the first door and went out to the courtyard. The gravel didn't hurt her feet even though she wasn't wearing any shoes. It was only when she stood still for a second at the final door that she felt a slight stinging. *My feet are bleeding.* It didn't matter.

Here she was at the final door to society. The door the customers came through when they entered the House. It was a door that she never used. Even when she moved into the House she'd come through the back door. And here she was. Death behind her. Freedom in front. She couldn't turn back. She couldn't look back. Without another thought, she threw herself at the final door, undid the hatch, and pushed it open.

Sparrow didn't know what the capital was like. She hadn't grown up in the city and the only time she'd gone through it—to be placed in the House—had been during the night. She knew it was a buzzing metropole with houses and coaches and pretty people. She remembered Nanfield's stories. What she expected, however, was not what she met.

Outside the walls, chaos ensued. People were running. Faces Sparrow didn't have a name for. Houses were burning and the whistling of bombs dropping sounded almost like the pianolotron.

"Why are you standing there?" A man yelled at her. "Run!"

He ran down the street and Sparrow followed without thinking. She wasn't as fast as him and he soon disappeared into the group of people that were all running the same way. Sparrow started to feel trapped with people all around her. *Where were they running? Out of the city? Back to danger?* She didn't know what was back and what was forward. On both sides of the streets, there were tall houses, making it feel like the street was fenced in. The air was thick with smoke, making it hard to breathe.

Another bomb hit, right in the middle of the group. People scattered, thrown in all directions. Sparrow flew into a back alley where she landed on some boxes with a hard thud. She scrambled to her feet right away, ready to go back to the main street, or maybe find another way. She couldn't just stay here. Pure animal instinct—wanting to survive— flooded her veins.

There was less whistling now, which Sparrow took as a good sign. Instead the air filled with groans, grunts, and screams. People were dying all around her. She helped a young man to his feet.

"Do you know the way out of here?" she asked. "I think we need to leave the capital."

"Yes." Blood ran down his face. "But I need to find my father first, will you come with me?"

Gunshots sounded.

"What the hell?" She whispered. "What is happening?"

38

Had the world been like this before she'd moved into the House? She couldn't remember. But what she could remember was more green than concrete. Now the ground was hard under her feet and she hadn't seen a single tree, bush, or pot of flowers, not that she'd notice anyway.

"It's the rebels," the boy said. "Come on." He waved at her to follow and they crawled down the alley to the other side. The houses here were made of wood, and one of them was on fire. Sparrow followed him.

It felt like the first couple of years at the House. Her body was paralyzed with adrenaline and fear. Her mind ignored any physical sensation of pain so that she could focus on the most important goal. Sparrow needed to survive. She wanted to live. It didn't matter what happened as long as she managed to live another day.

She watched the boy crawl onto the main road. He looked back at her, his mouth open as if to say something but nothing came out. Sparrow looked on in panic as he was shot four times in the chest. *Who was shooting?* The shots echoed in her head. Her eyes watered.

I need to hide. Now. I need to hide so that no one can find me. She registered footsteps marching closer but didn't see who it was, so instead she threw herself on the closest pile of bodies. She grabbed blood and mud and brought her hands to her face and her hair. After that, she lie very, very still. She willed her breath to soften and even though she couldn't calm her raging heart, she thought and hoped that they couldn't actually hear it.

In the corner of her eye, she could see them now. They wore black head to toe and had big brass rifles in their hands. *Are these the rebels?* Whoever they were, Sparrow knew that she'd never be on their side. She felt like stopping and spitting at their feet. Whoever they were, they'd destroyed her home and killed hundreds of people.

To her horror, the man closest to her aimed his rifle at one of the people on the ground and fired. She looked on as the others started doing the same.

"Please!" A female voice Sparrow couldn't locate rang out.

"Please what?" Another female voice answered. "I'm Deva of the Amelioratites, and I'm the one who will kill you." It was followed by a gunshot.

The shot echoed inside Sparrow's head. Clearly she wasn't the only one who had tried to hide among the dead. It was now or never; the people were coming closer. If she ran and they shot at her they might miss, but if she stayed as an unmoving target, only one thing that could happen. *The Amelioratites? Who are they?*

Sparrow bolted. She heard the voices behind her and several shots fired. How they missed her, she didn't know. A sharp sensation hit her shoulder and she staggered forward but her feet kept her running. She ran around a corner and fled into a cellar door, hoping that no one had seen where she went. She bolted the door and dove onto the floor. She went forward on her hands and knees until she found a cupboard. She opened it and crawled inside, the cupboard door closing behind her. It was uncomfortable, having her knees up and her head bent on top of them. But no one would look for her there, of that she was sure.

Her body ached in a way that it never had before and warm blood oozed down her arm. Had a bullet grazed her shoulder? Had she scraped it while on the ground? She wasn't sure. It hurt to breath, a sharp pain fell between her shoulder blades every time she inhaled.

I'm going to die here. A sob escaped her. She wondered how she was still alive. If she'd been a little bit slower down the stairs, the bomb would've hit her. If she'd been faster out in the street, the bomb would've hit her. She could've been shot many times. *I'm going to die here.* Maybe she would bleed to death. *Mama.* Sparrow had never felt so alone. Now that she was no longer in direct danger, she started to feel pain.

Please, please, please, please. Outside, the shooting had stopped and the whistling had begun again. Somewhere close a bomb fell and the ground shook. Sparrow screamed and fell out of the cupboard. She scrambled to her feet and ran to the door. *What did it matter to have a hiding spot if a bomb could kill you anyway?* She needed to move. *Now. Fast.* Anywhere was better than here.

With the bolt off the door, she ran back into the street, not caring that she still was barefoot. Above her, loud whistling cut through the rest of the chaos. Sparrow willed her legs to walk. She tried to run but couldn't anymore. The ground shook beneath her, almost knocking her to her feet, but she kept going. *Out of the city. I need to get out of the city. Now. Now. Now.*

The black dressed people were gone. Instead Sparrow spotted a few stragglers here and there. People who, just like her, survived the initial impacts. Sparrow didn't care about them anymore and she didn't follow anyone. Both for her own sake and for theirs. Each other time she'd tried to follow someone, they died soon after.

Her brain was quiet as she stepped over bodies and pushed people out of the way. She couldn't think about what she was doing or things she was seeing as she made her way through the little alleys, staying clear of the main streets. The whistling continued as she walked, and far away she could still hear gunshots.

In front of her there was a big house made of green bricks with a sign out front saying Moira's Wedding Attire. *Maybe I'm just walking in circles.* Sparrow stopped in front of it. She didn't know her way through the capital. What if she was walking deeper in? She was staying clear of the main roads and there were no signs for her to read except for *Moira's Wedding Attire.* She saw wedding dresses in the window. White like snow. White like bone.

Get moving again. When she stood still fear grabbed her heart again and she felt pain. She had to get further away before she rested. She continued past the store and down a small street that was lined with smaller houses, crammed side by side.

The whistling was further away now and she hadn't heard a single shot for a while. The sky was turning gray. The air smelled like smoke. Sparrow's walking had turned into a limp. She pulled her left foot behind her as she kept moving forward. She couldn't stop, wouldn't stop, shouldn't rest; not until she was outside the city borders.

"Help us." A woman sat on the steps outside a building, cradling a small child in her lap. Her eyes were wide and she was visibly shaking. She held out a trembling hand. "I can't move."

"I can't carry you." Sparrow limped over to them. She grabbed the woman's hand and pulled. "You can move. Come on!"

"Can you take him? Please." Sparrow chewed on the inside of her mouth. She was already tired. How she'd manage to carry someone else she d—

Voices made them both look up. Men in black suits were moving closer. One of them grabbed the rifle and aimed for them. Without thinking, Sparrow threw herself on the ground, bullets flying around them. She crept across the ground, then stood up and set off. How she was still managing to run, she didn't know. It was as if the rest of her body fell off. She didn't look back, but she didn't think the woman and the child had managed. If she had looked back, if she would've checked, she wouldn't have been able to continue.

There was no hiding now. All she could do was run. Her knees were killing her. Her feet had gone numb. A painful pounding in her abdomen told her she was in trouble and yet she ran with everything she had left. She could see a bridge now. A golden suspension bridge. Even though there were a couple of crashed carriages at the beginning of it, it was still intact.

Sparrow didn't slow down, not with freedom so near. She put her hands on one of the carriages and pushed but it didn't move. Instead she had to climb over it. The sea lay on both sides of the bridge and at the horizon the sky was turning from gray to light blue. Had this really lasted all night? Had it really been only *one* night? Sparrow felt like it was several lifetimes ago that she'd left her room and so closely escaped death.

The bridge was long and it took her quite a while to limp over it. She had nothing more to give. The further she got, the more pain she felt as the fear resided. Instead, anger brewed in her stomach. Who had attacked them? Who was evil enough to kill so many people?

Juliana, Henny, Eloise, Lolly... everyone dead. Madam Crowder had been gone before the attack. Had she known? Had she left them to die? Wherever Dolores was, had she survived? Had Nanfield died too? Sparrow didn't know if she'd left the capital or not.

The bridge ended at a big road. There was a sign attached to it, but the letters meant nothing to Sparrow's eyes. She turned around and looked back at the mayhem she'd escaped. Part of her couldn't believe this wasn't some twisted dream she was having. Soon she'd wake up and… no. Her body hurt too much for this to be a dream. The air was clearer here but she could still smell fire and gunpowder and underneath all of it, death.

Sparrow turned around and started limping down the street. She didn't know where she was going; she just knew she couldn't stay here. She needed to keep moving. Needed to… her energy was starting to fade. The ground was becoming closer. *Don't… do… it… have… to… keep… going.* Sparrow couldn't fight it any longer. Before she knew what was happening, she fell into one of the bushes and everything went dark.

Chapter Seven

Click, clack, click, clack, click, clack.

Voices. Talking. Hands on her body. Somebody grabbing her waist. Pulling. Pushing.

Click, clack, click, clack, click, clack.

"Welcome to Anchorage, little one."

Lights flashing above her.

The smell of morphine and soap. An injection in her arm.

"Is she dead? I think she's dead."

"I'm not dead," Sparrow muttered. She didn't know who was talking and she didn't care. She wasn't dead and she needed them to know it. She knew she wasn't dead. Otherwise, there was no way she would be in this much pain. She tried to sit up but somebody stopped her, placing gentle arms on her shoulders.

"Stay down, you're badly hurt. You're safe."

Sparrow tried to say something else but her mouth wouldn't cooperate. Instead tears sprung to her eyes, stinging her skin. A sob shook her body.

"Oh, little one." A cool hand touched her forehead, the only place where she wasn't hurt. "You've been through the mill, haven't you?" The voice held an accent that Sparrow couldn't place. It reminded her of another time.

"Where…?" She closed her mouth again as it hurt to talk.

"You're in Anchorage, the home of the revolution."

Was she at the home of the monsters who just attacked the capital and her home? She would never forget those people in the black suits, not for as long as she lived. She gritted her teeth. "The… revolution…?" *Damn you.* She wouldn't fight right now though. Not while they were helping her survive. Even in her half comatose state she could tell that a doctor was patching her up.

"Maybe she's a nationalist," another voice said. "Captain Tillgadd should've left her to rot. Just in case."

Sparrow opened her eyes, ready to face her enemy. An older woman stood over her wearing a white apron, a white coat, and the same visor as the doctor back home. Her eyes were gentle and her face was covered in wrinkles.

"Hush, Gwen." She smiled at Sparrow and cupped her cheek. "We let her recover first then we ask her what she is. And who she is aligned with."

Their gazes met while different emotions fought inside Sparrow. Eventually she closed her eyes again as tears pooled just below her cheeks.

"I'm going to give you something to make you sleep now, okay?"

Sparrow nodded. She was ready to never wake up again.

*

The sounds of whistling bombs and gunfire woke Sparrow up, her throat tight and her whole body shaking.

Blood rushed in her ears, making so much noise that it took her a moment to realize that it was quiet. There were no bombs. There was no gunfire. Just bubbling from some glass containers on the desk and the sound of air being pumped through a machine on the wall next to Sparrow's bed.

She felt better now, although she didn't know how it was possible. She felt very weak and tears sprung behind her eyes, ready to fall should she will them. But there was no sharp pain, only dull ache. Her body was healing. She propped herself up to sitting and looked around the room.

She was in a shack. A small wooden house only as strong as the nails holding the planks together. Wind made its way between the planks on the wall, rustling some papers on the desk. Covered in a thick pelt, Sparrow didn't feel cold.

She moved her toes, then her feet. They ached but felt fine. There were medical wraps on one of them. She didn't have the strength to reach down but her fingers touched anything she could reach without moving the rest of her body. There were bandages here and some stitches there. The scariest part was trailing her way up her left arm. She touched her left shoulder carefully. She remembered the pain as the bullet grazed her. She closed her eyes. She couldn't believe she was still alive. It felt like a miracle.

"Are you awake now?" It wasn't the old doctor from before. Instead it was a young woman. Sparrow recognized the voice from earlier. The one who had speculated that she was a nationalist.

She was short and chubby with a wide smile and twinkling eyes. She wore the same white apron as the doctor but no visor. She gave Sparrow a small smile and then looked at the machine next to the bed.

"How are you feeling?"

"I don't know. Alive." Her voice sounded rough. "Thank you for saving me."

"When Captain Tillgadd brought you here, I thought you were dead already." The little woman sat down on a stool next to her. "You almost weren't breathing. I told the doctor not to bother."

Sparrow raised her eyebrows. "Well, I'm glad you're not in charge then."

To her surprise, the woman laughed. "Me too," she said. "I don't want to be a doctor, and I definitely don't want to be in charge of who lives or who dies. I want to be a technician or an electrician but I haven't gotten the chance yet." Her smile was strangely contagious. "And I am glad that you're alive, alright?"

"Right." Sparrow could only look at her. A million thoughts ran through her head, the need to survive permeating everything. "I'm Sparrow, what's your name?"

"I'm Gwen. Nurse to the T.A.L.W. revolution. Led by General Dace. Our pride and joy." Her eyes twinkled again. "Do you feel fine to walk? We're going to have more wounded come in soon and you technically don't need this bed anymore. You can stay with the other refugees."

"Refugees?" *General Dace? Revolution? T. A. L. W?* Sparrow felt like falling asleep again. It seemed less complicated.

"Refugees, pilgrims, call them whatever you want," Gwen said. "They live in tents on the courtyard and soon you will too. Don't worry, everyone has access to the outhouse and gets one cooked meal a day, as long as you help out." She crossed her arms. "We're not a charity. We're the T. A. L. W." She pronounced it like a word, not like a string of letters as the doctor back home had.

"So I'm going to get to live in a tent," Sparrow said tentatively. She sat up and stretched her back and her arms. Her body was waking up which meant the majority of pain was coming back too.

"Listen," Gwen said. "I don't know what standards you're used to, but you'll get used to it soon enough. I know I did."

"I'm sure I will." Sparrow swallowed. She put one foot on the side of the cot, then the other. Somebody, probably the doctor or Gwen, had dressed her in beige trousers, thick moccasins, and a beige sweater. She was thankful for that. If she didn't have to see her bruises and stitches she could pretend they weren't there.

"Be careful." Gwen put her hand on Sparrow's shoulder. "Take it easy now, you've been heavily medicated. You'll feel strange when you get up."

Strange was an understatement. As soon as Sparrow's feet hit the floor, she faltered and swayed from side to side. A thick pain pushed her downward and she felt her legs buckle. She kept herself up with one hand on the bed and the other on Gwen's shoulder.

"Just stay still for a minute," Gwen instructed. "You'll feel better."

Sparrow stood still, holding on to Gwen as her world spun. She tried to breathe calmly but every time she did, she closed her eyes, saw terrible visions, and it started all over. She didn't know how much time had passed. Maybe only a minute. Maybe seven. Eventually her panic abated and even though she was still nauseous, she was able to stand on her own.

"Good girl," Gwen said. "Now come on." She led Sparrow out of the medical shack.

Anchorage, that's what they'd called it. Sparrow had expected a city of some sort but she wasn't sure what to call this. The medical shack was the first of many cottages and shacks and small buildings that made a U around a myriad of tents, too many for Sparrow to count. At the apex of the U, a church stood, tall and metal against the white, cloudy sky. At the church's entrance, flags waved. Sparrow couldn't read the letters this far, but guessed that they said T. A. L. W. Steam and smoke rose from the church's many chimneys. Beyond the buildings all Sparrow could see were dark forests. She turned around, eager to take it all in. Behind her, next to the medical shack was a set of stairs. Underneath the stairs there was a gate but on the other side of the wall, the turning blade told Sparrow that there were windmills. The air smelled fresh in a way that Sparrow had never experienced before. She took a tentative deep breath, ignoring the pain as she filled her lungs. She could smell trees. And water.

"Are you coming?" Gwen looked at her with an amused smile on her lips. "I know, I know… fresh air and all that. Take it in."

Her ears started working again. Anchorage was loud, almost as loud as the bar back home. People were talking. Children were playing. Somewhere close by she could hear a blacksmith banging on steel. A man shouted orders, loud enough so that she could hear him but not see him.

"This is Anchorage?" She caught up with Gwen who was walking along a path between the cottages and the tents. They were getting higher up, closer to the church. "This is…" Sparrow bit her lip before continuing. "This is the T. A. L. W." She tried to pronounce it the way Gwen did, like one word.

"In the flesh." Gwen flashed her a smile. "This is the quartermaster." They stopped by a black tent. In the opening another flag waved in the wind. Outside the tent, there was a little wooden table and in front of it stood a little man. A huge array of papers spread about the table with a big book holding them in place.

"Klaus, this is Sparrow." She turned towards Sparrow. "Sparrow, this is Klaus, Quartermaster at Anchorage. He will assign you a bunk and a task. None of that mooching here, right?"

"Right." Sparrow stared at Klaus. She'd never seen someone so short. His red beard didn't make him look any more normal.

"I have to go back now," Gwen said. "Come back for a check-up later, please? I'd hate for Dr. Teresa to think I kicked you out only to die." She looked like she was about to laugh. "So come by, prove you're alive." She winked at Sparrow and then headed back down the path.

"That nurse." Klaus shook his head. "People really have different ways of coping with trauma."

"Trauma?" Sparrow was starting to feel like an idiot. Her head hurt and she wasn't following. She needed more sleep. More rest. Maybe the world would make more sense then.

Klaus walked over to the table, got up on a little stool, and opened the book. The stool didn't help much and Sparrow could see that he was standing on tiptoe. He grabbed a pen and went down what looked like a registry.

"Full name, age, and skills."

"My name is Sparrow." Her head pounded and she closed her eyes briefly. "I'm…"

Klaus interrupted her. "Your full name please." His voice was nasally. "I need your last name, too."

51

Last name? Sparrow's head spun. She had one of those, right? She just hadn't heard it for several years. The last time she'd seen it was when her mother signed her over to Madam Crowder. Sparrow... Sparrow... She opened her eyes.

"My full name is Sparrow Stonehill." It almost sounded right. It'd been so long. "I'm 27 years old." She wasn't entirely sure about her age but she knew she was older than 22 and younger than 30. 27 sounded about right.

"That's two out of three." Klaus smiled to himself and scribbled in the book. "Now, what skills do you have?"

"Skills?"

Klaus blinked. "Yes, skills," he said. "You heard Nurse Gwen. Everyone helps out. Even the children have their age-appropriate tasks."

Sparrow felt her face heat. She'd never felt so useless. What could she do? Steal cherries? Scrub kitchen floors? She'd rather die than suggest that she could tend to the physical needs of Anchorage's leaders.

Klaus sighed. "Can you clean bird cages?"

Sparrow nodded. "Yes. I think I can."

"Good." Klaus scribbled a last note and closed the book with a thud. "That shall be your task then. General Dace uses pigeons and magpies and maker knows what else to communicate with the rest of the T. A. L. W. No one lasts long on bird cage cleaning. So we're all grateful that you're willing to give it a try."

Things were happening too fast and her pounding headache and nausea made it hard to understand what she was agreeing to.

"Shelter?" She had no other words left. She felt herself swaying.

"Of course, of course." Klaus jumped off the stool. "You're in luck; we have a free tent for you to sleep in." He started walking with short, quick steps. Sparrow hurried after him, faltering every other step. "If you'd have come two days earlier I would've had to set you up in the same tent as a family of six, and good luck getting any rest in there."

"Yes. Thank you." People were everywhere as they walked among the tents. They greeted Klaus with nods and hellos but mainly ignored Sparrow. For that she was grateful. She just wanted to get into her tent and lie down on whatever was in there.

"Ah. Here we are." They slowed down. "This is number 56."

Number 56 was a small, elongated tent made of red tarp. It sat on the edge of the tents and there were less people here, more privacy, less talking.

"I get to sleep here?" Even the ground looked inviting.

"The tent is yours alone until we get more refugees or if someone more important who needs it comes." Klaus licked his lips. "And when it gets colder, you can come back for a thicker blanket. Maybe I'll have one available then. I don't have one now."

"Okay." Sparrow felt the world shrink. "Thank you."

"Yes, yes." Klaus turned away from her. "Good luck." He left her with a few quick strides, as fast as you can be when your legs were as short as Klaus's.

Sparrow didn't look at him and she didn't look at the people who were looking at her. She got down on her knees and crawled into her tent. Inside, there was only a kerosene lamp and a bedroll. On the bedroll lay a moth eaten blanket and a pillow covered in a stained pillowcase. It looked like absolute heaven. Sparrow crawled forward. She was asleep before her head reached the pillow.

Chapter Eight

When Sparrow woke up she felt a little bit better. Her head no longer hurt and the various cuts and bruises on her body itched rather than ached. She took that as a good sign. It still hurt to take deep breaths and her feet still felt on fire. She wasn't completely better but she was getting there. More important than anything, she was alive. *And at the hands of the T. A. L. W.* Sparrow gritted her teeth. She needed to know if the rebels had staged the attack on the capital. And if they had, she needed to leave. She sat up and crawled out of the tent.

It was evening now. Here and there, fires lit up the night. Somebody was playing a guitar, sad songs that Sparrow didn't know. Somewhere out in the dark, a woman was crying. It still hurt to walk but Sparrow managed. She walked past some of the tents and people looked at her.

"Do you want some?" An older woman held up a bowl to her.

Sparrow looked into the pot over the fireplace. It looked like porridge but smelled better than anything she'd ever been served at the House. She took it. "Thank you," she mumbled.

"You can sit here if you want," a little girl sitting on a tree trunk said.

"Thank you." Sparrow walked over to her and sat down. She took a spoonful of the porridge and almost placed it in her mouth when yells made her look up.

"They're back! They're back!"

The sound of rolling chains told her that the gate was opening. She set her bowl on the bench and got up. The guitar strumming stopped and the sound of hooves filled the air. Three horses trotted on the path from the gate to the church building. Sparrow's heart started pounding and her eyes refused to focus. Brown leather pants. A breastplate of brass. Rifle on her back. A hood covering most of her face with some blonde strands curling outside.

Astrid got off her horse in one fluid motion and handed the reins to a young boy wearing the same armor as her. The other riders got off their horses, too. Klaus came over to them, talking and carrying the large book. What Astrid answered, Sparrow couldn't hear. She was too far away.

Her feet started carrying her forward. *I should have known.* Sparrow hadn't connected it before. The secrecy. The armor. The rifle with the words *To arms, liberate Waerdarei.* T. A. L. W. How Sparrow hadn't put two and two together, she didn't know. Now she just needed to figure out what Waerdarei meant.

"Wait," she said. But no one heard her. She willed her feet to move faster.

Astrid was moving too fast towards the church. Sparrow didn't want her to go through the door. If she did, Sparrow would lose her.

Sparrow made her way past her tent and was now out on the path. She faltered and almost tripped over a rock. "Wait." But her voice was now a whisper. She was so small. A nobody. And Astrid hadn't even noticed she was there.

Astrid was nearing the door, still not looking back. Sparrow jumped forward, almost reaching the door when a hand grabbed her shoulder and pulled her backwards. He'd touched the shoulder where the bullet had grazed her and the pain made her see stars. She fell to her knees with a whimper.

"What are you doing?" A voice behind her asked.

Sparrow looked up. It was another man in armor. She stood up again, touching her hand to her shoulder.

"I don't know who you are," the man said. "But General Dace and the others just came back. They're not to be disturbed."

"General Dace?" Sparrow's mouth felt dry.

"Are you daft?" The man shook his head. "General Astrid Dace is the leader of the rebellion. If you have any complaints, take it up with Klaus or one of the others. But the general and her captains are not to be disturbed by any of the refugees."

Sparrow's heart stood still. Next to the church white flowers grew, she fixed her gaze on them while trying to figure out what was going on. General Astrid Dace. Not to be disturbed.

But I know her, a voice inside her said. *We've slept in the same bed. I've prepared baths for her. She kissed me.* That kiss, no matter how small and chaste, still made her cheeks heat up.

"Okay." She nodded. "I apologize."

She turned around. She still wanted to speak to Astrid—she had too many questions not to—but she wasn't going to do it while the others were around.

*

The radio was on in the medical shack while Doctor Teresa muttered over a tub of bubbly water cleaning medical instruments. A voice on the radio blathered on.

"Earlier this afternoon, Chancellor Rathmore denounced these horrible attacks that plagued the capital during the night before yesterday. Luckily the Chancellor's own family had been on their annual trip to the coast and no one in the royal family was harmed. He has made a promise to find and punish those responsible. After speaking to the nation, he went straight into another mee—"

"Gwen," the doctor said through gritted teeth. "Just turn that drivel off."

Gwen walked over to the radio and saw Sparrow standing in the doorway.

"Look who came back, doctor." She clicked the radio and it went silent. "Our miracle patient."

The doctor turned around. Her smile was gentle.

"Hardly a miracle," she said. She took her gloves off. "No broken bones." She went over to Sparrow, put an arm around her shoulders, and moved her towards the cot. "Sit down." Sparrow listened. "The majority of the healing you did yourself." She pushed on Sparrow's shoulder until she lay down.

"I feel fine," Sparrow said. "Well, my shoulder and my feet."

"Your feet look like minced meat."

"Gwen, you're not helping." The doctor pushed the nurse away. "No, they don't." She shook her head at Sparrow, probably trying to comfort her but it had the opposite effect.

"Yes they do." Gwen grinned. "But looks don't matter, right? You can clearly still walk."

The doctor looked exasperated but Sparrow lifted the edge of her chin. Gwen was right.

"I actually wanted to know a few things." Sparrow winced when the doctor took the moccasins off her feet. She sought the doctor's gaze instead of looking down even though she could hint at something red and blue at the edge of the bed.

"Yes." The doctor nodded. "I'll answer your questions as well as I can. Gwen, grab some of the numbing cream from the counter."

Sparrow closed her eyes and gritted her teeth, waiting for the pain that would come with the doctor treating her feet. "Where am I?"

"You're in the stronghold of the T.A.L.W." The doctor spoke slowly. "Anchorage we call it. Our safe haven. A place where we can be free. A base for..." The doctor touched a point on Sparrow's big toe that made her wince. "Sorry."

"Who is Waerdarei?"

Both Gwen and the doctor stopped still and looked at her.

"What?" Sparrow looked at them both. "Did I say something bad?"

"You must be younger than you look," the doctor said. "Most people over 20 know that Waerdarei is the name of our country."

"It is? Which country is that?"

"Told you." Gwen curled her upper lip. "A nationalist. She had to be right in the inner sanctum to not even *know*."

"What are you talking about?" Sparrow had never felt so lost. It felt as if she spoke a different language. "This is Rathmoria Emporie, right? Did I cross a border?"

Gwen snickered.

"Stop laughing." The doctor let out a deep sigh. "The letters in T.A.L.W," she said, "stand for *To Arms, Liberate Waerdarei.* Waerdarei being the original name of our country before the Chancellor changed it."

Sparrow's head spun. On one hand, it felt like new information, and on the other hand, it felt like she'd already known. She'd been born in Waerdarei, she'd sung the national anthem, waved the sun-yellow flag of the country she loved. She'd forgotten. She'd forgotten all of it.

"What about General Astrid Dace?" *Who is she?*

"She's the leader of the T.A.L.W." The doctor started to clean her feet and the room smelled of disinfectant. "She's the one who founded this place, together with some of her most trusted friends. What started as a small group of insurgents in a basement in the capital has grown to a group of thousands of people who have an army, that—"

"That bombed the capital!" Sparrow felt tears in her eyes. She didn't know how she could feel so disappointed in someone she didn't know. "How could General Dace do that?"

The doctor let go of her feet.

"General Dace had nothing to do with that vile attack! We don't have access to those kinds of bombs or air force. There's no way we could've carried out such an attack." She threw her hands in the air and moved so that her height was in line with Sparrow's head. "And you will do well not to speak like that." The gentleness in her face was gone and sharp brown eyes met Sparrow's. "Those are lies from a Chancellor that attacked his own capital. Blaming it on us to sew hatred and anger in his people's hearts."

"Really?" Sparrow met the doctor's energy. "And why the hell would he bomb his own city? I was there. He must've lost thousands of his own civilians. What's the point?"

The doctor took a deep breath. "Because he is evil." Her tone was calmer. "And we scare him. The T.A.L.W. has tripled in size during the past year alone. He's losing his grip and when a psychopath loses control, they lash out."

Sparrow shook her head. She'd never heard anything but good about the Chancellor. There was a portrait of him on the wall in Madam Crowder's room. Or there was, she supposed. Probably nothing hung on her wall now. It didn't exist anymore.

"I…" Sparrow didn't know what to say. She buried her face in her hands. A memory arose, one that she'd almost forgotten, a voice, a shooting. "What are the Amelioratites?" The woman had also said a name, but Sparrow couldn't remember it anymore.

The doctor spat on the floor. "Don't say that name here."

"She's serious," Gwen said. "And that rule goes for all of Anchorage. Don't mention *them* or their schools anywhere around the T.A.L.W."

"What?" Sparrow looked at the doctor first and then at Gwen. "I don't even know what I'm saying! If I'm not allowed to mention them, I can't ask about them. How will I learn?" It was an honest question. She was growing irritated with all the secrets she didn't know.

"It's okay." The doctor placed a hand on her head. "It's a scary world out there and I know not everyone from the capital knows what's happening in the rest of the country. Now let me look at your shoulder."

Sparrow snorted but complied. It was clear that neither the doctor nor Gwen were going to answer her questions. She hadn't known what happened in the capital either. She knew nothing. She'd never known anything.

Chapter Nine

When Sparrow left the medical shack this time, it was night. Some of the fires still burned but others had gone out. Her stomach reminded her that she hadn't finished the bowl of food that woman had handed her before. The doctor would know where she could get food. She almost turned back, but something stopped her. Sparrow was embarrassed. Her own ignorance had never mattered before.

She looked at the sea of tents in front of her. It was empty now. Most people were sleeping and there were only groups here and there that talked in hushed tones. Further away, the church rose like a menacing shadow. Somewhere in there, Astrid existed. In her mind's eye, Sparrow had no problem imagining Astrid talking, sleeping, taking a bath. She remembered her sharp eyebrows, cold blue eyes, full lips that never seemed to be properly smiling. Sparrow knew what she smelled like. How could she know what someone like that smelled like when she herself was just a common street walker?

She started walking the path, letting her feet find the way and her mind relax. The windows of the church were still lit up and the flags were still out. Sparrow walked over to the door and put her hand to it. It reminded her of all the other doors that divided her world in the past. The front door to the outside. The Madam's door. Any door that led to rooms where she wasn't invited. *No more.* She curved her fingers around the door handle.

She pulled. *Nothing.* She pushed. *Nothing.* The door was locked. And whatever was inside was not for Sparrow.

For a moment she played with the idea of knocking. Maybe if someone answered she could say that she was looking for General Dace. Surely if she said... Sparrow let go of the handle. She'd seen enough of this camp to know that everyone seemed to worship Astrid. No one would let Sparrow near her. She sighed.

"What are you doing?" One of the guards stepped out of the shadows. "The church is closed. Go back to your tent."

"Nothing," she snarled. For being a haven, they sure were impolite to the people they were supposed to welcome. "Good night."

She left the guard by the door and went back to her tent. Tomorrow would be a new day.

*

The next time Sparrow woke up it was daytime again. Sunlight streamed through the tent's opening and the smell of fried eggs and sausage permeated the air, even inside. Sparrow recognized the smell from another time and her mouth watered. She sat up and dusted off the same clothes she'd fallen asleep in. *Maybe I can get new clothes somewhere.* She'd never worn the same outfit more than a day without washing it and she was starting to feel gritty.

She moved her fingers and toes, touched her shoulder, and took a breath of relief. Her body really was healing and before long she knew she'd feel normal. By then she'd know what she wanted to do. If she wanted to stay or leave. *Leave to where?*

Sparrow discarded her loose thoughts and crawled out of the tent. Outside, the day had already started. All over the place people were eating, their plates covered with eggs, sausage, and vegetables Sparrow didn't recognize. She didn't remember the last time she had had eggs or any type of meat. Women and men had placed big metal plates over the fires and a long line formed past Sparrow's tent and almost to the church.

Not everyone was eating. Next to Sparrow's tent, a woman sat on a bench. She held a blade and was cutting her hair, tears streaming down her face.

"What are you doing?" A strange wish rose in Sparrow. A wish to *help*. She sat down next to the woman and looked at her.

"They need bow strings." The woman refused to meet Sparrow's gaze. "The blacksmith can turn my useless hair into strings."

"Oh...." Sparrow licked her lips. "Why are—"

"Hcy, new girl." Klaus appeared out of nowhere, carrying the big book again. "Sparrow, was it?"

"Yes?" Sparrow got up. She threw a look at the woman but then focused on Klaus. "What is it?"

"You promised to clean the cages, didn't you?"

Oh right. Sparrow swallowed. "I guess I did, yes."

"They're expecting you in the church where Captain Kane will show you to the room where the birds are kept. Have you had breakfast?"

"No." Sparrow's stomach gurgled again and she put a palm to it. "I'm hungry."

Klaus looked like he was about to explode. While Sparrow looked on, he grabbed a stick from the ground, stuck it into one of the sausages, and then handed Sparrow the stick. The skin of the sausage sizzled and Sparrow felt her mouth water.

"Eat that as fast as you can and then go to the church." He only looked at her for as long as it took her to nod, then turned to the other side. "Gretchen, can you please…"

Sparrow ignored him. She hadn't thought about her job yet but now Klaus's words drummed up energy. The church. She was going to get to work *inside* the church. She blew on the sausage. She wanted to finish it when she got to the church door.

It was open now and without any hesitation, Sparrow swallowed the last piece of sausage, threw the stick on the ground, and went inside. The walls were made of stone and the steam pipes hung on the wall rather than inside the walls, like Sparrow was used to.

"Are you Sparrow?" A tall man with dark bushy hair stood in the corridor. He wore the same armor that Sparrow associated with Astrid.

"I am."

"Fitting name," the man said. "I'm Captain Kane. Please follow me."

He led her through the corridor, the air thick with incense. It was quiet, apart from muted conversations somewhere in the house.

"Are there still religious services going on here?" Sparrow hurried to keep up with him.

"Yes," Kane said. "But only once a month. Then we invite everyone to the main hall in here." They left the corridor and walked through the main hall. It looked like the churches Sparrow remembered, pews of benches and an altar in front. The room was empty. "This is where you go to get to the birds." They walked through another door next to the altar and then up a curved staircase which led to a small room.

The walls were made of wood and on one of them, several cages stood on top of each other. There were magpies, doves, and a couple of falcons. One of the cages held sparrows. On the other side there were wooden boxes and a desk. Sparrow was itching to take a look at the papers but tried to listen to Captain Kane instead, pretending like she wasn't spending all her energy looking and listening for Astrid.

"Uh huh." She nodded. "Clean them with the brush. Put fresh wood shavings on the floor of the cage. Fill water and food." She'd been listening more than she knew.

"I shall leave you to it then," Captain Kane said. "Will you find…oh General Dace, I'm sorry."

Sparrow turned around. Her heart stopped, she held her breath, and goose bumps rose on her arms. At the top of the stairs, oh so close, stood Astrid. She wore brown leather trousers and a white shirt, no breastplate and no hood. A few buttons of her shirt were open, revealing the soft-looking skin of her upper chest.

"It's okay, Kane." She smiled and nodded. "No worries. I find it easier to think up here, with the birds." She threw a fond look at the birds and then her gaze landed on Sparrow. Her eyebrows rose slightly.

"If you need to use the room, general," Kane said quickly, "I can ask the girl to come back."

"I'd actually like to do it now," Sparrow said. She wasn't going let people speak like she wasn't there. Not anymore. Never again.

Captain Kane stared at her with a horrified look in his eyes. Astrid looked amused.

"I'm so sorry, general," Captain Kane said with his head lowered. "I had no idea she was going…"

"Oh, just let her finish," Astrid said. She waved at them both dismissively. "I'll be at my desk. She'll be over there." Without giving Sparrow another look, she sat down at the desk.

Kane looked at Sparrow, his facial expression saying *behave* in more ways than one. Sparrow shrugged at him, turned towards the cages, and lifted the bag of bird feed that stood on the floor. She listened to his footsteps. As soon as he'd gone down the stairs, and the door had opened and closed, she dropped the bag and walked over to Astrid.

Astrid leaned over the papers, looking at something intently, but when Sparrow came closer she looked up again. There was no recognition in her dead eyes but Sparrow knew that she recognized her.

"So you made it out of the capital." It was a statement, not a question.

"Barely," Sparrow said. "None of the others did."

Astrid sighed and straightened her back.

"I didn't know it was coming," she said. "If I had, maybe I would've warned you."

"I don't like that you put a 'maybe' in there." Sparrow crossed her arms over her chest. "I didn't know you were a general."

"And how would you?" Astrid turned back to the papers. "I purposely didn't tell you."

Sparrow chewed on the inside of her cheek. It shouldn't have hurt but it did. *It was just a business transaction. I've had hundreds of customers and Astrid was no different.* Even though she had felt different.

"You're safe here." Astrid said without any emotion. "We have plenty of refugees already. Plenty of resources and everybody helps out. It's not the most comfortable life but I'd say it's better than what you're used to."

Sparrow stared at her. How Astrid could sound so cold was unbelievable. "I should take care of the birds," she said.

Astrid nodded without looking up.

Fine then. Sparrow didn't know what she'd been expecting. She went back to the cages. How hard could it be? She knew Klaus had said that nobody wanted to keep this job for long but maybe that was because of the snooty general that treated everyone like…. Sparrow sighed.

She panicked when she noticed that the bird cages had no doors.

"Um, Astrid?" She turned around.

Astrid twitched as if somebody had pinched her.

"It's General Dace," she muttered. "What is it?" She still had one of the papers in her hand.

"What are you reading?" Sparrow's curiosity got the best of her.

"None of your business," Astrid said. "Did you need help with something?"

"What does the T.A.L.W. *do?*" She hoped that her question wouldn't make her angry. "I know that they fight against the Rathmore family. I know that you're trying to bring down the empire, but how?"

Astrid looked up from her paper without putting it down. "We try to strike military targets only, but sometimes civilians get caught in the fire." She scratched the top of her head. "Do you have any more questions? I can't tell you everything, for security reasons. I'm sure you understand."

Sparrow nodded. She did have one final question though. "How do I open the cages?"

Astrid threw her another look, sighed, and put the paper on the desk. She stepped up next to Sparrow and leaned down.

69

"Here," she said. "The mechanism is underneath." She took a hold of Sparrow's wrist and held her hand underneath the cage to where Sparrow's fingers touched the mechanism. The cage sprang open.

"Thanks." Sparrow felt mortified. Maybe she should hurry and get out of there as soon as possible. She reached inside the cage, stretching for the small bowl, intending to fill it with food.

"Don't, they will—" Astrid started but it was too late. The big crow inside the cage had already jumped forward and sunk its beak into Sparrow's palm. Sparrow yelled and pulled her hand back, almost making the cage fall to the ground if Astrid hadn't been there to stop it from toppling over. Astrid closed the cage as Sparrow held the wound close to her mouth and blew on it.

"You idiot." But Astrid's tone was soft. "We have enough problems as it is without losing our birds." She took a deep breath. "They aren't pets. You need to be careful."

"I'm sorry," Sparrow whispered, feeling her face burn.

"Nobody taught you this." Astrid grabbed her hand and held it up to look at the wound. "How would you know how to do it? Come here, a crow's bite is easily infected. At least it's shallow."

She went over to the table and rummaged through a small metal crate that stood there. She got out a small cloth and a bottle, and held out her hand, waving for Sparrow to give her her wrist. Her hands were calloused and strong. It made Sparrow feel small. She inched as close as she dared. The bottle contained disinfectant that stung when it reached her skin, but Sparrow knew that it would clean the wound so she forced herself to stand still. When Astrid was satisfied, she took the cloth and quickly tied it around Sparrow's hand.

"There. Good as new." Their gazes met and Astrid's smile seemed genuine for once. "Take care of the birds. Just don't put your hand inside the cage."

"How am I supposed to do anything without putting my hand inside the cage?" Sparrow definitely knew why nobody else wanted to do this.

"You let the bird come out and sit on your shoulder first," Astrid said. "Then without the bird inside, you can do whatever you need and want with the cage."

"They won't fly away?"

"No." Astrid's smile was a proud one. "I trained them not to."

Sparrow looked back at the myriad of cages. Cleaning all of them would take her hours. She was terrified of going near the bird again but between them and Astrid, the general was scarier. Sparrow moved closer to the cage. She opened it, moved her shoulder to the opening, and like Astrid had said the bird climbed out and sat on her shoulder. It was heavier than she'd expected it to be and its claws dug into her shoulder. *Good thing I didn't offer my hurt shoulder,* she thought as she cleaned the cage and then filled it with both water and food. When everything was done, she leaned her shoulder back towards the cage and to her joy, the bird willfully went back in and Sparrow snapped it shut.

Before moving on to the next cage, she looked back at Astrid. Now more than ever, she didn't know who she was. A general. It was a general of the revolution that had held Sparrow against the wall. It was also a general who'd offered her to sleep in the same bed. It was this very general that had kissed her. *That had happened, right?* So many things had happened since then, Sparrow wasn't sure if she'd made up the memory.

Cleaning all the cages took hours. Astrid stayed at the table. Occasionally reading, occasionally writing. Occasionally she paced around the room. Sparrow started to sweat and her clothes were spotty with bird food, wood shavings, and things she didn't want to identify. It felt like half the day had passed when she finally closed the last cage. She looked around. Astrid was now sitting on the chair, leaning back, deep in thought.

"I'm done," she said.

Astrid hummed in reply.

"You're really scary," Sparrow whispered. Before Astrid had a chance to answer, she walked down the stairs. It was time to leave the church.

Chapter Ten

Sparrow dug her heel into the dirt on the ground outside her tent. She'd never been outside the capital, and even though it occurred to her how strange it was that she'd never seen earth before, it was a fact. She looked at the lump she gathered on the top of her shoe. It was brown, grainy, and had a single strain of grass. Sparrow looked at the woods growing behind Anchorage. What would the ground look like there?

She was standing in the queue for breakfast, early enough that she'd have time to eat both the egg and vegetables. She had learned over the past week that the earlier she was, the longer time she had to eat. She'd also learned that taking time to eat breakfast, savoring food while talking to the people around her; that was real freedom. She wore a fresh bandage around her shoulder and her feet were almost healed.

She refastened the belt around her tunic and put her fingers to the small flowers engraved all around the belt. It was still just two days ago that Gwen had come out of nowhere, seen how dirty she was, and showed her how to bathe and where to get new clothes. The seamstress wanted three gold coins for the tunic, the trousers, and the shoes and Sparrow wasn't sure how to make any money.

"Thank you." Her mouth watered as she accepted the plate from Helena, the woman who cooked at the fire closest to her tent. Instead of sitting down, she took her plate over to Captain Kane who stood guard by the church entrance.

"Good morning." He nodded slightly to her, keeping his gaze on everything else. He wasn't fond of her, Sparrow knew that. Not since the way she had talked to Astrid. She wondered if it was thanks to him or Astrid that she hadn't run into the general again since the first time.

"I have a question." She forked some food and chewed it before continuing. "How do we feed all of these people?" She wasn't good at estimating but there had to be at least 150 people at Anchorage. "I've been offered food more than once a day every day. Where do we get it? Is there a huge farm somewhere that I'm not seeing?"

"We do have some livestock," Kane said. "But mainly we rely on donations. There are even some rich families who supply us with what we need."

Sparrow nodded. "Another question then. If one wanted to earn a few coins, what would one do? I understand that everyone has a job and they do it to help out but some of the services offered require money. I came here with none."

He looked at her from toe to head. "How much do you need?"

"Five gold coins." *It's always good to have a little bit of extra.*

Kane sighed and walked over to her, lowering his voice. "There is something you can do for me. But I'm unsure if…" He bit his lip.

Oh no. Sparrow's throat went dry. *All men are the same.* Her heart started a staccato rhythm; she couldn't believe she'd been so stupid to actually ask.

"The church is overrun by rats."

"What?" Sparrow dropped one of her eggs on the ground. "You want me to kill rats?" She looked inside the church, almost expecting to see a rat running across the stone tiles inside.

"Capture them, kill them." Kane shuddered visibly. "We just want them gone." He straightened his shoulders. "I don't like the idea of them being killed but I want—I need—them gone."

Sparrow bit her lip to stop herself from chuckling.

"Okay. I'll catch some rats for you."

"After you take care of the birds," Kane said.

"*After* I take care of the birds," Sparrow agreed. "Are there any cages I can use?"

"No," Kane said. "But if you turn right instead of going across the main hall, you'll find a corridor of spare rooms. Some of these are unused and full of scrap parts. Wires, boxes, scrap pieces of metal. Use what you need to build traps."

Sparrow smiled at the thought of a new challenge. Who could've known that life was allowed to be like this? Full of new experiences. She'd get the money to pay off the seamstress and she'd still have two coins to spare. In her mind, Sparrow was already walking around the stands by the cottages, looking for ideas on how to spend it. There were several vendors who sold different wares around the camp for coins. She couldn't wait to look closer.

"We have a deal."

Captain Kane looked relieved.

*

It was lunch-time when Sparrow was done with the birds and headed back down the stairs. She went through the main hall and turned right like Kane had said. It didn't look unused like he said though. T.A.L.W. flags hung on both sides and the floor was brushed. Sparrow didn't really follow the politics around the rebellion. She was too focused on her new freedom. She was content in not being responsible for the fight. But this corridor, the flags, the atmosphere; it was humbling to step into a place that smelled like authority.

Some of these are unused and full of scrap parts. Wires, boxes, scrap pieces of metal. Use what you need to build traps. That's what Kane had said. She was starting to feel a bit worried about not finding any rats though. Maybe they were in the cellar? Provided that Sparrow could even find her way there.

A sudden sound made Sparrow look to the side. A person was behind one of these doors. Even though she knew she shouldn't, Sparrow had to investigate. She walked over to the door from which she thought the sound came from. She'd barely had time to press her ear against the wood when the door was forcibly pulled open and Sparrow fell forward, landing in the arms of Astrid.

"I'm sorry! I'm sorry." Sparrow tried to catch her balance. She found quickly that she could only stand up straight by grabbing a hold of Astrid's arm, otherwise she would've fallen.

With her face turning the color of blood, she stood up straight and looked up at Astrid's face. Astrid was wearing her full armor and the look on her face was completely unreadable. The side of her face was red and raw.

"What are you doing here?" Astrid's tone of voice was very low.

"Captain Kane is paying me to catch rats." Sparrow looked behind Astrid into the room. The room was empty except for a large table. A big map was spread out on the table. *Stop looking.* Sparrow turned her gaze back to Astrid.

"Look at me for a second," Astrid said.

Sparrow looked up and properly into her eyes. Astrid's gaze bore into her with an intensity that stole Sparrow's breath. A blue fire danced in the depths of her eyes. Sparrow didn't know how somebody could look so beautiful and deadly at the same time. Neither of them said anything for a long while. Finally, Astrid seemed satisfied and her gaze softened.

"You act too suspicious for your own good." She shook her head and left Sparrow by the door. She went over to the map and brought one hand up to her chin. "If you didn't look so innocent, one would think that you're up to something."

"Captain Kane said that the rooms on the right were empty." Sparrow had to defend her actions. "That they were full of spare parts to help me catch the rats."

"If you turn right when coming into the church, yes." Astrid chuckled. Sparrow hadn't heard that noise since Astrid had come to visit her in the House. "You must have been coming from the main hall."

"Oh." Sparrow felt like an idiot. "I think you're right."

"You'd make a really terrible spy." Astrid threw her a look.

"I'm not a spy," Sparrow said. She didn't know what to do with her hands. Did she always feel this awkward?

"No." Astrid looked like she was amused. "You're a prostitute. And a rat catcher."

Sparrow sucked in air through her teeth. *How dare Astrid talk to her this way?* "Rat catcher will do." Sparrow looked down at the ground. Why did she allow Astrid to talk to her this way? It didn't matter that she was a general.

"Tell me, rat catcher..." Astrid made Sparrow look up again. "...if you were an evil dictator who had just attacked your own capital what would your next step be?" She mindlessly scratched her own cheek. "After blaming the only people daring to stand up to you."

"I..." Sparrow shook her head. "I wouldn't know."

Astrid turned her head to the side. "Are you saying you don't have an opinion or that you just don't want to share it?"

Fine. "Is beating the revolution an option?"

A fire lit in Astrid's eyes again and she nodded her head violently. "Never."

"Then I'd catch a couple of rebels," Sparrow said. "Or a scapegoat to prove to my people that I can show quick results."

"That's what I'm thinking too," Astrid said. She took a deep breath. "Or use the situation to enforce even more laws. Most people choose safety over freedom. Go back to your duties, rat catcher. They're probably in the cellar."

"Thank you." Sparrow turned around. She was about to close the door when Astrid spoke again.

"And Sparrow?"

Sparrow looked at her. If she could memorize Astrid like this, cocky, amused, and beautiful, she would. It was a strange thought in the midst of all the chaos.

"Don't let me catch you in here again, yes?" Astrid smiled with the side of her mouth. "If I do, I might actually think you're a spy."

Chapter Eleven

"Gwen?" Sparrow didn't want to bother the doctor with something silly but her hands had several rat bites and it was probably good to have a medical professional look at them.

The two beds in the medical shack were occupied. A man wearing the T.A.L.W. armor lie in one, his eyes closed.

"I'll be right with you." Gwen was standing next to him, fiddling with something attached to his arm.

The other bed carried a young girl who was covered with burns from head to toe. The doctor was giving her an injection and didn't look up when Sparrow came in.

She didn't want to be in the way so Sparrow stayed by the door. The bites on her hands were itching and she did her best not to touch them.

"Stop being such a drama queen," Gwen told the man. She gave his arm a squeeze and went over to Sparrow. "Come on, let's talk outside."

They went out of the medical shack and Gwen pushed her down on a rock.

"Let me see." She held out her hand and waited for Sparrow to put her hand in it. "Wait, these aren't bird bites. These are... rats?" She chuckled. "Did Captain Kane put you up to this?" Her eyes glittered.

"How did you know?" Sparrow winced when Gwen took a wipe from her apron and touched it to the bites.

Gwen chuckled again. "Because he came in last week with the same type of bites."

Sparrow couldn't help but chuckle too. That's why he seemed so ashamed when he asked. Maybe somebody even higher up had tasked him to do it and instead he had managed to pawn it off on her.

"How much did he pay you?" Gwen asked.

"Five gold coins."

"You should've asked for 10. Wait here." Gwen went into the medical shack. In a bit she came back with a couple of bandages. "They have a huge problem with rats in the church. Around the tents, too. It happens when so many people gather in the same place."

"What's wrong with the people inside?" The thought of such a young girl being hurt....

"The girl was in the capital." Gwen didn't meet Sparrow's gaze. "Her mother died bringing her here."

"Will she survive?" Sparrow worked very hard to not think back on the night of the attack. And everyone she left. Everyone who died.

"I don't know." Gwen sighed. The glitter in her eyes disappeared and she looked older for a moment. "That's why I told the other guy in there that he was being a drama queen. Sure, both his legs are broken but at least he's not a child who was burnt to a crisp and just lost both her parents and her home."

"I guess." Sparrow started to feel uncomfortable with the topic.

"You should've seen General Dace," Gwen continued, peaking Sparrow's interest. "The doctor wasn't here so she went to get me. Her eyes were wide, her face red." Gwen moved both hands up and down. "She came running into the medical shack. Ordered me to grab any tools I could and follow her." She sighed. "I got to sit behind her on her horse and we galloped down the road."

Sparrow couldn't help but feel jealous of Gwen sitting so close to Astrid. "I don't know how the general found her, but there she was. I'll never forget that sight. The mother was dead but in her arms, the girl was still alive. Hurt, but alive. The general looked furious and heartbroken in the same time. She let me ride while she carried the girl all the way back to town."

"When was this?" Sparrow's mouth had gone dry.

"Late last night," Gwen said. "You know, I hear stories of the general's big heart and how she cares. I mean, otherwise she wouldn't have started the T.A.L.W, but it's really something to see with your own eyes."

"You didn't say to just let the girl die as well, did you?" Sparrow asked. "Like you did with me?"

"Oh, don't be like that." Gwen shook her head. "This was a child. A child that the general herself saved. You were a straggler, brought in on a cart together with other bodies. I wouldn't have gone through who was alive and who was dead if the doctor hadn't explicitly ordered me to."

"Oh." Sparrow hadn't known the specifics. "I wasn't aware."

"You're not supposed to be aware of that," Gwen said. "I shouldn't have told you at all."

"It's fine." Sparrow swallowed. "I'm alive, aren't I?" She liked Gwen—she did—but she wasn't alive thanks to her. She turned her head to the side. "Gwen?" She had to ask the question. "Can you please tell me about the Amelioratites?" She lowered her voice to a whisper on the last word. "I promise I won't mention it to anyone else, I just have to know."

Gwen's smile disappeared. She looked into Sparrow's eyes for a moment and then groaned.

81

"Okay, fine. When the Chancellor closed the regular schools, he opened schools all over the country called Ameliorate Institutes. Not everyone gets to attend, only the best and the brightest from the right families." Gwen rolled her eyes. "And you know what that means. Once you've gone through that education since childhood, when you've been under *that* kind of indoctrination, there's nothing left but pure obedience. These are the people who make up the Amelioratites. The Chancellor's special force." Gwen pursed her lips. "And that's all I'm going to say on the subject. Ask me about other things instead. Please."

"Gwen!" The doctor stuck her head out of the door. "Why are you out here? I need you."

"Duty calls." Gwen got up from her place next to Sparrow. "I'll tell you more another time, okay?"

Sparrow watched as Gwen went back into the medical shack. Then she got up from the rock.

Food was cooking by the fires. Porridge with herbs made with real milk. Sparrow liked it enough. It was better than the food she'd been offered at the House. But the coins were heavy in her pocket and she knew that the vendors had other things to sell.

She walked up the path from the medical shack. She stopped and plucked one of the flowers that grew on the side of the path and fastened it in her hair. She didn't walk among the tents like usual; instead she walked between the cottages and looked at the different vendors that had set up shop.

Maybe this is what it would've been like to walk in the capital before the attack. Sparrow felt herself questioning things she'd never questioned before. *Why* hadn't they been allowed out of the House? What threat had there been, making it so that they could only stay inside, just servicing others with their bodies until… Sparrow's heart skipped a beat. She'd forgotten them. The women who'd come before.

Margene, who'd been in her 30s, and one day just disappeared. Nanfield had said she moved but why would she have left without saying goodbye? Tonya, who held Sparrow every night to help her sleep when she'd just come to the House. There were more. Nadine. Olga. Elin. Others that Sparrow didn't know the names of. All of them had one day been gone. All of them had been older than Sparrow. They all couldn't have left without saying goodbye. Without saying where they were going.

Sparrow's feet led her to a fruit vendor and she stared at a bowl of cherries. The thought of them all disappearing, all being discarded like trash. Sparrow swallowed back nausea. What else hadn't she thought about during her life?

"How much?" She pointed at the cherries.

"One half-coin per hectogram."

Sparrow didn't have any half-coins but instead of asking for change, she asked for two hectograms. To her delight, he poured the entire bowl of cherries into a leather satchel and handed it to her. She paid him one of the coins and took the bag.

A small trail behind two of the cottages took her from outside the U-shape of Anchorage and the forest above. From there the trail went upwards until she found herself on a cliff next to the church. She sat down, dangling her legs over the edge. She needed to come here again. The stone was warm under her trousers and she could see all of Anchorage from up here. It looked like a doll encampment with dolls going about their business.

The gates to the stables next to the church opened and some people led horses. Sparrow didn't need to see them properly to know that it was Astrid who rode in front. She sucked on a cherry while watching them ride out of Anchorage. *I wonder where they're going.* Sparrow wasn't worried that Astrid wouldn't come back; she was just curious. She was curious about a lot of things. She was a citizen and she didn't know anything about the country she called home.

Chapter Twelve

Something was wrong. Sparrow opened her eyes. Her tent was dark. Someone was screaming. *Had they been attacked?* Sparrow's shoulder twinged, reminding her of what had happened during the last attack. Sparrow needed to move. She needed to get out. She needed to leave before the whistling and the shooting started. *Now, now, now.* Finally her body cooperated. She twisted around, scraping her knee in the process. She crawled out of the tent.

Outside, she assumed it would be chaos but instead it was mostly empty. The air was filled with snoring that could've given Madam Crowder a run for her money. Sparrow searched. She hadn't woken up for nothing. She knew she hadn't.

A light was on by the medical shack. Sparrow darted forward, her feet keeping up with the rhythm of her heart. This wasn't an attack like on the capital, this was something else. But Sparrow needed to know what.

She slowed down when she was near the door, but instead of pressing her ear against it, she opened it carefully and slipped inside. She didn't need to hide in Anchorage and she wasn't embarrassed for being curious. The sights that met her stopped her heart.

On one of the cots, Astrid was sitting. Blood oozed out of a fresh wound on her side. Her mouth was open in pain. On the other cot, where the girl had been lying, a sheet covered the shape of her. *She hadn't made it.* As sad as Sparrow was about the girl, she couldn't shift her focus from Astrid.

The general looked up when Sparrow entered. The doctor looked over her shoulder from her place next to Astrid.

"Please leave," the doctor said. "If you need help, I can assist you in the morning. Gwen isn't here right now."

"No." Astrid's gaze met Sparrow's. Her eyes were dull and darker than usual. "It's fine, she can stay."

The doctor shrugged and returned to stitching the wound on Astrid's shoulder.

Sparrow walked up to her. Astrid's lips were pressed into a pained grimace and her free hand curled around the mattress of the cot. *She's in pain.* Without thinking, Sparrow put the pads of her fingers to Astrid's strained hand. She gave it a small caress. Astrid glanced down at her hand, then back at Sparrow. Something in her face gentled. Then the doctor put the needle in and she groaned again.

"What happened?" Sparrow whispered.

"We were ambushed." Astrid croaked. "The Chancellor's men took Isabe—" She cleared her throat. "Captain Tillgadd." Sparrow almost giggled. It felt like another lifetime ago that Isabeau and Astrid had both visited her. She remembered how Isabeau hadn't wanted Astrid to say her name. How Sparrow had assured them that the name Isabeau meant nothing to her. *Well now it did.*

"Do you think they'll kill her?"

"Of course not," the doctor interjected. She put her tools on the metal plate. "There, all done."

"I don't think they'll kill her either," Astrid said. She put her shirt back over the tank top with pained, jerky movements. When she struggled with the front buttons, Sparrow pushed her hands away and started buttoning them herself. Astrid didn't stop her.

"It's me they want," Astrid said through gritted teeth. "They know how I feel about her." *Oh.* "They know she's like a sister to me." *Phew.* The strange feelings of jealousy quickly dissipated. "They know that I can't do this without her."

"You will do just fine, General." The doctor said. "You will make sound decisions. You will keep up the fight."

Astrid nodded but Sparrow saw the grimace she made. She wanted to grab Astrid's hand again. She wanted to comfort her. Tell her she believed in her. She put her hands behind her back, just in case she got any strange ideas.

"I should get back to the church," Astrid said.

"You need to sleep," the doctor said. "Take the pills I gave you before you go. And you." She pointed at Sparrow. "You shouldn't be here at all. I don't know why the general said it was fine for you to stay."

Astrid threw her a glance.

"We know each other from outside Anchorage." Sparrow wasn't going to hide anymore. "I was worried about her."

Whatever Astrid had been expecting, it wasn't that. Was that a hint of a smile? Sparrow couldn't tell.

"Fair enough." The doctor didn't ask anymore, and for that Sparrow was grateful. "But I'm going to bed." She went to the farthest corner in the room, reached for a metal handle on the wall, and pulled. Down sprung a readymade bed.

"Goodnight doctor," Astrid's tone was back to normal. Royal and assertive. "And thank you."

She opened the door and made a gesture for Sparrow to walk through it.

Fresh night air met them and above, stars twinkled. It had to be really late because none of the fires were burning and usually somebody was up playing an instrument half the night. It seemed as if all of Anchorage was asleep.

They started walking up the path, not between the tents but sticking next to buildings. Neither of them spoke at first. Sparrow was dying to ask Astrid what had happened. *How* were they ambushed? Would Astrid *manage* without Isabeau? Could Sparrow do anything to help?

"I found a cliff earlier," Sparrow said in a hushed tone.

"Oh?" Astrid kept her gaze forward.

"If you go between the vendors here." Sparrow pointed. "There's a trail that goes behind the houses and takes you to a cliff. From there you can see everything. All of Anchorage. I saw you ride out from there." She smiled. "While eating cherries." *And spitting the pits at Anchorage down below.* But Astrid didn't need to know that.

Astrid chuckled. "Well I know you like cherries," she said. "Show me."

"What?"

"Show me the trail. Show me the cliff. I'm not ready to go to bed."

"Astrid." Sparrow loved saying her name, especially since she seemed to be the only one that used it. "It's dark."

"I have good night vision, come on."

Before Sparrow had a chance to protest, Astrid turned between the vendors and found the trail that Sparrow had pointed at. Before losing her to the dark, Sparrow darted forward and grabbed a fistful of Astrid's shirt from behind. Astrid didn't say anything so Sparrow kept her grip on her shirt as they made their way through the dark.

The scents were so much sweeter at night. Night-blooming flowers, the wet smell of earth, spicy pine. It all filled Sparrow's nostrils and created a heady scent that made Sparrow question if this was really happening. Astrid moved with fluidity, her back warm against Sparrows knuckles, not like someone who'd recently been injured. Twice, Sparrow almost tripped over roots on the trail but then the trees became sparse. When they reached the cliff, there were no trees.

"Oh maker," Astrid breathed.

Before them, Anchorage spread out. The dark church cast a soft shadow and the tents looked like white and brown dots. Above it all, the dark blue sky twinkled with stars and two full moons. It was as if someone had turned a marine bowl over all of it. Sparrow couldn't remember the sky ever looking so big.

"This is…" Astrid looked back at Sparrow, her eyes twinkling. "Thank you for showing me. I understand if you wanted to keep this to yourself."

"I don't mind sharing it with you." Sparrow looked down, needing to break eye contact. If she kept it, Astrid would know. She would know what Sparrow wasn't ready to admit to herself yet. "Come on." She walked slowly towards the edge, careful not to step too close.

She didn't know where the bravery came from, but she sat down, dangling her legs over the edge like she'd done earlier that day. Astrid came and sat down next to her, groaning as she put pressure on her shoulder to get down. Silence fell between them as they looked at the view.

Astrid sighed. A sad sound.

"I'm sorry about Isabeau," Sparrow said. "I remember her. I could see the friendship between you."

"We're like sisters," Astrid sighed again. "I need to help her."

Something glistened on her cheeks but Sparrow didn't dare to think that Astrid was actually crying. An owl shrieked somewhere in the night.

Astrid took the pills out of her pocket and threw them into her mouth. She swallowed soundly.

"Why did you kiss me?" Sparrow had wanted to ask that for a long time now. Astrid hadn't seemed interested in her body any of the times she'd visited so why, *why,* had she kissed her that final night at the House?

Astrid snickered, the sound unexpected. Sparrow knitted her eyebrows and stared at her. What was so funny?

"Your lips look kissable, that's all."

"Oh." Sparrow touched her finger to her lips. It was such a small comment and yet it made her feel things she couldn't remember ever feeling before. "But did you—"

Her words were drowned when Astrid turned toward her, grabbed a hold of her nape, and pulled her in for a kiss. Sparrow moaned as Astrid's warm mouth attacked hers, a wicked tongue finding its way inside. Sparrow couldn't remember ever being kissed like this. So thoroughly and with emotion. Tears landed on her cheek but she wasn't crying. Astrid was. Sparrow cupped her cheek, her hand becoming wet. Astrid bit her lip, causing Sparrow to whimper. She pulled away.

"What are you doing?"

Astrid leaned forward and licked the side of her mouth. The action caused lightning to fly inside Sparrow. She was breathing hard.

"I want you. Please." She leaned forward again but Sparrow stopped her.

"I'm not a prostitute anymore." Sparrow needed to say it. She needed Astrid to know.

"I know that," Astrid said. "I still want you." She took off her leather jacket and threw it on the ground, away from the edge of the cliff. "Let's get away from the edge."

Sparrow traced her hand around the curve of Astrid's jaw and let it travel up into her hair. She grabbed a handful of blonde strands and pulled. Astrid groaned but Sparrow could see her smile in the dark. "I'm doing this because I want to," Sparrow whispered. "You need to know that."

"Sure, rat catcher."

Sparrow needed to wipe that cocky smile off Astrid's face. She couldn't stand it. She let go of Astrid's hand and moved backwards until she reached Astrid's leather jacket. She lay down, looking as Astrid moved like a cat towards her. The thought that this general wanted her made her dizzy and her heart beat fast. Astrid held herself above her, the azure fire in her eyes threatening to burn her up.

"Kiss me." *Please.* Sparrow's mouth was dry.

Astrid relaxed her arms and let her whole body lie on top of Sparrow. Their bodies aligned and Sparrow squirmed; it was as if her body was on fire. Astrid didn't move. She just stayed on top, looking at her. Their breaths mingled. *What is Astrid looking for?* Sparrow knew she was fully clothed but she felt naked. Before she had a chance to react, Astrid started rocking and moving against her.

"You feel so good." Astrid pressed a little kiss beneath Sparrow's ear. She rocked harder and made a whimpering sound as if her frantic movement against

Sparrow's mound was nowhere near enough to push her over the edge.

Sparrow was trembling as she put her hands on Astrid hips. She made a shushing sound. "I'll help you." She pressed a quick kiss to Astrid's forehead. "Let me help you." Sparrow wasn't very smart. She wasn't good at reading. But this she could do. This she could help with. This she was good at. And the thought of truly discovering the heart of Astrid made her mouth water.

The look in Astrid's eyes was more than urgent, as if she was in pain.

"Turn around." She tugged on Astrid's hip and moved so that Astrid was on her back.

They were still outside, stone underneath them and the starry night above. The night was cold. They couldn't take their clothes off. Sparrow lay down next to her, head leaning against her hand, and pressed against Astrid's side. She let her hand wander, cupping her breasts, kissing her cheek.

"Please." Astrid said again and closed her eyes. She chuckled. "I don't even know what I'm asking for."

"I do." Sparrow pressed a gentle kiss to her lips. "Don't forget to breathe."

She pressed one last kiss to Astrid's cheek and then crawled down the way of Astrid's body. She undid the buttons on her leather trousers and placed a gentle kiss on top of the blonde curls she found there.

"Oh maker." Astrid put one of her arms over her eyes. "What are you doing to me?"

Sparrow put her fingers around the top hem of Astrid's trousers. "Up."

As soon as Astrid let her, Sparrow pulled her trousers down to her knees, making sure the jacket was underneath her so that none of the rock touched Astrid's bare skin. She inhaled deeply. She couldn't believe what she was about to do or that she wanted it so much.

She leaned in and tentatively licked the length of her. Astrid's chest rose and fell but otherwise she didn't move. It was as if she was worried that Sparrow would stop if she moved. Sparrow smiled against Astrid's flesh when she saw that the only part of Astrid that moved was her toes, stretching. Maybe they were even curling inside her shoes.

"Make me come, make me come, make me come, make me come." Sparrow heard above her and doubled her effort. She brought one of her hands up and entered her with one finger and then two, eager to feel Astrid's warmth while never stopping the movement of her tongue. With a heart wrenching cry, Astrid came and pulsed in Sparrow's mouth.

Astrid went limp underneath her, breathing deeply. Sparrow couldn't help but place one last kiss on the tempting lips just under her mouth. She was incredibly turned on herself but every time she squeezed her hips all they met was rock and it didn't give her any relief. She knew there was nothing to give her relief and she moaned against Astrid's flesh in her own desperation.

Still unmoving, Astrid started breathing calmly and Sparrow moved up her body. Astrid's eyes were closed and her even breathing told Sparrow that she'd fallen asleep. Sparrow stared at her. *Unbelievable.* Sparrow had never had sex by her own will before but she was quite sure that it wasn't supposed to end like this. Sparrow rubbed her legs together, feeling her own wetness and excitement. Astrid had barely touched her; Sparrow couldn't help but feel cheated.

She reached down and pulled Astrid's trousers up as much as she could. Leaning her head on her arm, Sparrow settled next to her. She closed her eyes, curled up next to her general, and forced sleep to come.

*

A fly buzzed near her ear and Sparrow swatted at it. Her arm hurt like a mother and she grimaced. Where was she? She opened her eyes. Clouds floated above her, casting shadows on the rock. The events of last night came back. *The medical shack. Astrid. Walking up here. Sharing the view. Their...* Sparrow sat up. She was alone. Whenever Astrid had left, she left her jacket and tied it around Sparrow's waist to keep it from opening and leaving Sparrow cold.

I can't believe she left. A single nightingale was singing somewhere close. Sparrow closed her eyes. She felt like she'd been through a mill. Her body wasn't made for sleeping on such a hard surface. She wanted to sink into a hot bath. Sooner rather than later. She got up and walked over to the edge, looking down at Anchorage. And there, not far away at all, Astrid was walking through the sea of tents, heading to the church.

We slept all night together. Sparrow smiled, a tension leaving her shoulders. The sun was still rising and most of the fires hadn't been lit yet. The line to the bathhouse didn't look very long yet either. People were getting up, getting ready for their jobs and assignments. Klaus was running through the tents too, carrying that book of his with him. Sparrow almost chuckled. Anchorage was a strange place. A strange place full of nice, caring people who had survived the worst. Who saw all the ill will in this world and said "no more." Sparrow knew that there were things to learn. Things to decide on. She still hadn't properly taken a side. She also knew she would one day soon.

Time to go. Time for bathing, for breakfast, and then she would take care of her birds. She folded Astrid's jacket with care, stroking out any creases. She hung it over her arm. It didn't feel right to wear it. She started walking down the trail and headed back.

Chapter Thirteen

During the next couple of days, Sparrow almost questioned if she'd imagined the whole thing. The one time she met Astrid in the corridor of the church, just passing by, Astrid paid her no attention. Sparrow kept her jacket on her bedroll in the tent. She didn't want to bother Astrid and felt it was better to keep her head down. Astrid had bigger things to worry about.

Something was going on. Plans were set in motion. The church was full of people, walking back and forth in the corridor Sparrow wasn't allowed to enter. Riders came every day, carrying letters for the general or weapons for the army. The T.A.L.W. was planning something. Something big.

One morning when Sparrow walked up to the birds as usual, Astrid was standing there talking to two of her captains. She flashed her a quick look when Sparrow came up the stairs but didn't seem to think of her as a threat. She faced her captains again.

"We can still turn this to our advantage," Astrid said in a confident tone of voice. "Don't worry about her." The captains must have looked questioningly at her.

Sparrow tried to ignore them as she walked over to the cage and got to work.

"Are you sure?" One of the captains said. "The thought of sending someone in there, someone without a weapon, without support…"

"And yet that's what Captain Tillgadd would do for any of us." Whatever Astrid was talking about she seemed very sure.

Stop listening. Sparrow was really trying to focus on cleaning out the cage. But to stop listening was impossible.

"Fine. Just tell me when she's ready to leave."

The captains left.

Sparrow had one of the magpies on her shoulder and was just about to fill the food bowl when Astrid spoke. "How much of that did you hear?"

"All of it." Sparrow helped the magpie back into the cage and closed it. She turned around.

Astrid was leaning against the table, her arms folded. "You couldn't help but listen, right?" Astrid looked more amused than anything else.

"Well," Sparrow said. "You were talking in my presence. It's not my fault."

Astrid snorted softly. Then her face turned more serious. She kicked off the table and walked up to Sparrow.

"I have a job for you," she said. "If you're willing."

Sparrow couldn't help it. She chuckled.

"How big are the rats this time?"

Astrid shook her head, smiling. "Sadly it's just one big rat."

"Do I have a choice?" Sparrow turned to the next cage, helped the bird out and started cleaning it on autopilot. "Or do I have to accept it for the good of the T.A.L.W?"

"I don't know." Astrid kicked some stray bird feed with her boot. "Do you have a choice? Could you live with yourself if you said no?"

Sparrow looked at her for a moment but Astrid's face betrayed nothing. It was strange to think that the last time they had interacted Sparrow's lips had been wrapped around her. "What kind of job?" Sparrow looked away. "It better not involve any fighting or killing or…" She swallowed. "I don't want to be in danger."

"You will be in danger," Astrid said calmly. "Just living here puts you in danger. Look at me." She waited until their gazes met. "Doing what we did together that night puts you in danger. Do you understand that?"

Sparrow nodded. She turned around and put the jackdaw back in its cage.

"I want you to join the Chancellor's household." Sparrow dropped the bag of birdseed as she spun around. "As the son's girlfriend."

"Girlfriend?" Sparrow's mind raced. "What the hell do you mean?"

"The son has trouble making friends and anything else." Astrid spoke calmly. "The country is starting to wonder why he doesn't have a woman by his side when he is well within his 30s. My spies have informed me that the Chancellor is trying to set him up. Find him a respectable woman."

"And you think I'm…" Sparrow pointed at her own chest.

"Don't be ridiculous." Astrid waved her hand dismissively. "Not you, rat catcher. Not Sparrow. But Amelie Dartmoor might. Daughter of Lord Dartmoor. A girl of society. A bit shy perhaps. That's why she's still a virgin and has no suitors. But she is very beautiful."

"I'm not," Sparrow felt her cheeks heat. "I'm not, you know."

"Beautiful?" Astrid's eyes twinkled.

Sparrow wanted to shove her.

"I'm counting on Rufus Rathmore not knowing enough about women to notice whether she's a virgin or not."

Sparrow started to feel sick. What gave Astrid the right to sell her?

"Do you expect me to sleep with him?" *I thought you were different.*

"The only thing I expect you to do is listen," Astrid said. "And watch. Rufus will spill everything if he thinks a woman likes him." She sighed. "Find Isabeau and the others. And should you find something else out in the meantime that's a bonus."

"What if something happens?"

"Then something happens." She sounded so matter-of-factly that Sparrow wanted to throttle her. *Didn't she care?*

"What will I do if something happens?" Sparrow knew she needed to continue to the next cage but she stood frozen to the ground.

"Then you'll figure it out," Astrid said. "You'll be in the inner sanctum. Following the family. Protected by the same guards that protect the family."

Sparrow looked at the birds. She thought of her name. *Sparrow.* Did it matter that she was human? "I'll just be another bird to you."

Astrid followed her gaze. "Perhaps." She touched her finger to one of the cages. "But your cage will be prettier than theirs."

"I don't know anything." Sparrow needed Astrid to understand. "I have never lived anywhere except for the House where you met me. I don't know what the Chancellor has done. I don't know why T.A.L.W exists. I don't know anything."

Astrid's gaze softened. "I know. I'm hoping that will help. It'll keep you from lying."

"Okay." Sparrow nodded. "I'll find Isabeau for you." How could she say no when the thought of finding Isabeau lit Astrid's eyes up? When it made her look more alive than any other time? "But I won't sleep with him." She stared at Astrid. The right to set her own boundaries was paramount.

"Yes." Astrid gave a curt nod. "I'll ask Captain Fordon to take you to the Chancellor's summer house tomorrow."

"You're not taking me there?" Sparrow's heart pounded.

The size of what she'd agreed to was starting to dawn on her. She was going to leave the safety of Anchorage. She was going to leave Astrid. And she was going to walk straight into the beast's mouth. *For Astrid.* Sparrow pursed her lip.

"Of course not." Astrid walked over to the window and looked out. "I can't leave my post and I definitely can't be the one to deliver you. I'd be recognized. I'm also on another mission."

"Another mission?"

"I won't tell you the specifics, of course." Her smile could only be described as devious. "It's something that will *tip the scales* if you will. But don't worry," Astrid said as Sparrow walked over to her. The window overlooked the forest behind Anchorage. "Every agent out there is my eyes and my ears and my rifle. Whatever happens to you, I will know within minutes. Wherever my people are, so am I. They will keep you safe for me."

Sparrow swallowed. Fear was gathering in her depths and she hoped it wouldn't take over.

"I don't know whether you are stupid or smart."

Astrid's words hurt her. She didn't want Astrid to think she was stupid. "What do you mean?" Sparrow asked.

"You don't ask what I think you'll ask." Astrid started rolling her thumbs. "You don't know much about T.A.L.W like you said. I receive questions and worries from everyone, but not from you." She scrutinized Sparrow. "Don't you care about what's happening? Don't you want to know?"

"Do you want me to ask questions?" Sparrow looked at Astrid's thumbs. "Do you want me to worry?"

"Do you want to ask me anything?" Astrid turned towards her fully, resting against the wall.

Sparrow instinctively knew that this was an opportunity not given to many. Whatever she asked right now, Astrid would answer. And if Sparrow really was allowed to ask anything, she didn't have to think even for a second what it would be.

"Who are you?"

"I'm Astrid." Astrid's eyes were so blue. They shone so bright that the rest of the world fell away. "Or General Dace. Take your pick. Do you need to know more than that?"

"Maybe not." Sparrow itched her scalp. "Did you have a pet growing up?"

This made Astrid laugh. "I had a badger."

"A badger?"

Astrid nodded. "I called her Fiona and she was my best friend. Affectionate, clean, and smart. We weren't allowed pets in the convent so I felt lucky." Her face carried a dreamy expression. "The gamekeeper accidently shot the mom, put her babies in a bag to drown them but gave one of them to me."

"You were raised in a convent?" Sparrow asked.

"By nuns." Astrid nodded. "But that's a story for another day."

Sparrow had a thousand more questions now, but some of them she couldn't even begin to find the proper words for. How an orphan raised by nuns had grown up to lead a revolution as a general was a mystery. Other questions lurked in the back of her mind. *Why did you give me a job? Why me? Why did you sleep with me? What would you say if I told you I find you beautiful?* Sparrow swallowed. "What happened to Fiona?"

"She died of old age." Astrid looked out the window again. "I buried her somewhere in a forest just like this one."

Clouds were gathering outside and it looked like it was about to start raining. Sparrow didn't want to leave. None of them knew what would happen in the future. Maybe Sparrow would never return. Maybe Astrid would die while she was away. Maybe Sparrow would die. It was possible that this was the last time they'd ever talk to each other.

"You scare me." The statement said more than any question she could have asked.

"I am good with a weapon," Astrid said. "And I lead a revolution. I have friends in high places. It's only natural that you'd be scared of me."

"That's not what I mean." Sparrow touched her fingers to Astrid's glove-clad hand. "I wonder if you can smile, properly. I wonder if you know who you are. It scares me to think that you might've forgotten."

Astrid gazed at her, her eyes widening. She looked quickly back at the window. "Captain Fordon will meet you by your tent at dawn." Astrid cleared her throat. "She will bring bags for you to pack your belongings and proper clothes for you to wear. A girl called Bianca will come with you as your chambermaid. She can get a message to me if you need. Captain Fordon will also call you once a week on the telephone pretending to be your mother."

"Telephone?" Sparrow didn't recognize this word.

"Yes, a telephone. It transports voices through wires." Astrid shook her head. "Or something like that. I'm not an engineer. I'm sure your Madam had one in the House."

Sparrow nodded. Perhaps Madam Crowder used to have one. That didn't mean Sparrow had ever seen it. "Sounds fine."

Astrid cleared her throat. "I can take care of the rest of the birds." She put her hand in her pocket and pulled out two gold coins. "Why don't you buy yourself some more cherries? Enjoy yourself for the rest of the day."

Sparrow accepted the coins. *Come with me,* she wanted to say. She wanted to take Astrid out of the church. Out of Anchorage. Up on the hill where they could both be themselves and where Astrid didn't have the burden of the world on her shoulders.

"You'll do well, rat catcher." Astrid said. "Good luck tomorrow."

Chapter Fourteen

It was still dawn when a woman stuck her head into Sparrow's tent. She had short, spiky, black hair and dimples on both side of her cheeks. She was wearing the T.A.L.W. breastplate like the rest of them but hers seemed to be made of softer material that followed the lines of her body better. Sparrow had been awake when Captain Fordon came and it took quite a few minutes to see what set Fordon apart from Astrid and the rest. It was only when Fordon tried to smile with authority that Sparrow realized what it was. Fordon was younger. Much younger than Astrid. Probably younger than Sparrow. Maybe closer to Dolores's age.

"Good morning, ma'am." Fordon threw her a leather satchel. "Pack what you want to bring because you may be gone a while. And don't—I shouldn't have to say this—bring any weapons."

"I don't have any weapons," Sparrow said. "Wait outside, so I can get dressed."

She didn't want to show Captain Fordon that she was sleeping naked in the bedroll with General Dace's jacket wrapped around her body.

"Of course." Fordon disappeared and went outside.

It was time. Sparrow had enough sense to realize that this was probably the last time she'd sleep in this very tent. When she left somebody else would take over this one and should she ever return she'd be assigned another. She grabbed the satchel and put Astrid's jacket inside. A few days ago she had also bought a brush which she now placed in the bag next to spare underwear and socks. It was strange to think that she still didn't own anything else. The bedroll wasn't hers. She only owned one set of clothes; the medical clothes she'd given back to Gwen. *They know I don't have any proper clothes, right?* Sparrow couldn't help but assume that Astrid would've thought of providing her with clothes fit to meet the Chancellor's family. She touched her fingers to Astrid's jacket. The elusive general would probably not approve of her taking the jacket into the home of the enemy. But Sparrow didn't care. She needed that part of Astrid with her. Otherwise she couldn't stand it.

Captain Fordon was standing outside with her back towards the tent as if keeping guard. The sky was gray and most people were still sleeping.

"Ready?"

Sparrow nodded.

"Good." Fordon started walking towards the gate with quick steps. Her legs were longer than Sparrow's and Sparrow had to move in quick strides to keep up. "Kane should have the horses ready by now."

"We're going to ride?" Sparrow's heart jolted. She'd never ridden before. "I don't know if I can ride."

"Good that you don't have to do anything then." Fordon grinned. "The horse will do the job. You just have to hold on. I'll ride first and hold your bag."

They passed by the medical shack. No lights shone in the window. *It really is early.* A fleeting sadness passed through Sparrow. She hadn't had a chance to tell Gwen she was leaving.

Outside the gates, Captain Kane was waiting with two horses, both of them brown and big with stubby legs.

"Give me your bag." Fordon held out her hand and Sparrow gave her the bag. "Help her up."

Before Sparrow had a chance to react, Captain Kane had led her to one of the horses. He put his hands together and gestured for her to put her foot in them. She grabbed the horn on the saddle with one hand, put her foot on Kane's hands, and he projected her up.

"Put your leg on the other side."

I'm not an idiot. Now that Sparrow was up, she could kind of figure out what to do. She put her feet in the stirrups and gathered the reins.

"Feels okay?" Fordon mounted her horse too, keeping Sparrow's bag between her arms in front of her.

"Yes."

"Good." Fordon smiled approvingly. "Then you don't need to do much. I'll go in front. Your horse will follow mine. We have a few hours before stopping so there's plenty of time for you to get used to it."

Without waiting for Sparrow to reply, Fordon made her own horse walk on. For a second Sparrow panicked, but then the gentle brown beast underneath her followed. Fordon had been right; Sparrow didn't need to do much other than hold on.

The sun was still rising as they moved further and further away from Anchorage.

*

Sparrow didn't know how long they'd been riding. She just knew that the horse's steps were getting more and more tedious. Her butt ached, her back hurt, and she was very thirsty. She knew that horses could go faster, so why were they going so slow? In the first hour or so, Sparrow had been taken with the outdoors and the nature they passed. She'd never been outside the capital before and on the way to Anchorage she'd been unconscious. There was so much to see. Trees and bushes. Big rocks. Signs with letters Sparrow couldn't read. They passed small houses. Some abandoned, some lived in. Sparrow was so curious. She wanted to stop at every house. Talk to the people who lived there, ask them how it was to live in this country. However, they'd been riding through a thick forest for a long time and it was getting monotonous.

As if reading her mind, Fordon slowed down and placed her horse so that they walked next to each other.

"Are you still holding up okay?" Fordon looked as comfortable as a flower on a mountain, following the swaying of the horse's body.

"I'm a bit tired," Sparrow admitted.

"I understand that," Fordon said. "One more hour and we'll make a stop. Then you'll get to eat and drink and rest. You'll also get proper clothes fitted for the Chancellor's future daughter-in-law. Then we'll continue."

Sparrow nodded. They were crossing a stream. In the streams, yellow fish played.

"Fordon?" Maybe this was a perfect time to get some answers.

"Yes?" Fordon stopped her horse from getting in front again.

"Why are there so many captains? There's General Dace, but it seems like everyone at Anchorage is either a refugee or a captain. That's a bit strange."

Fordon chuckled. "I know," she said. "At first it's very strange. But it makes sense when you think about it. General Dace is a general because she's our general. She has to be more than a captain. But the rest of us, we're captains of our own destiny. We've stepped out of the path that the Chancellor chose for us. So we're all captains. All capable of greatness."

It did make sense, Sparrow supposed. She'd wondered about that for a long time. Especially since it seemed the captains didn't command anything.

"So how does…" She was about to ask another question when Fordon spoke.

"There's a small army of refugees though who refuse to call themselves captains," Fordon said. "They're recruiting any capable adult and training them to be part of an army. Ready to march on the capital or AngelGarden as soon as General Dace gives the command."

"AngelGarden?" Sparrow held the horn of the saddle when her horse took an extra large step over a rock.

"It's where you're going later today," Fordon said. "It's the holiday home of the Chancellor."

Oh. "Fordon?"

"Yes?"

"What has the Chancellor done that's so bad?"

Sparrow knew that she'd asked a very stupid question when Fordon pulled her horse to a complete halt and turned around in the saddle to look at her.

"What do you mean?" She sounded a bit breathless. "What do you mean 'what has the Chancellor done?'"

Sparrow almost bit her tongue. She didn't know what it was. If it was the dimples in Fordon's cheeks or the way her eyes still shone with youth and innocence.

"I know I should know more than I do." Sparrow started braiding the part of the horse's mane she could reach. "But I feel like I don't know anything and there's no one I can ask." She looked into Fordon's eyes. "I was brought to Anchorage. I didn't seek it out."

"What about before?" Fordon held her gaze, steady.

Gosh I like her. Fordon was as steady as one of the horses. Sparrow hoped they could maybe be friends when all this was over.

"I was a prostitute." Sparrow had never talked about herself so openly before. "I was sold by my family I think. I'm not sure. I was eight when I left my home. The Madam she sold me to let me work in the kitchen for a few years before graduating me to a full worker. I wasn't allowed to leave the House. We weren't allowed to socialize and the only people we ever met were paying customers." *I'll leave Astrid out of it. No one has to know.* "One night we were bombed. I ran out in the street for the first time in almost 15 years. Suddenly I was in Anchorage." She swallowed. "I know I must sound very ignorant but this is my truth."

Sparrow looked down, fixing her gaze on one of the lava rocks underneath. She could feel Fordon's gaze burning the top of her skull.

"Does General Dace know this?" Fordon's tone was careful.

Sparrow looked up and gave a short nod. "She's the only one who knows," she said. "I don't think she cares."

"Good." Fordon's careful grimace broke into a smile. "This is awesome! I've always wanted to teach somebody about why the T.A.L.W. exists!"

Sparrow laughed nervously. She'd not been expecting such a happy response.

Fordon kicked her horse in the sides and both horses started walking forward.

"Okay, there's a lot of material to cover but we should have enough time until we get to Nana's house."

Sparrow chuckled. *Nana's house?* She kept quiet though and listened to what Fordon had to say.

"Chancellor Rathmore was elected into office about 40 years ago," Fordon started. "He won the second political election through his party *People For Justice*. PFJ has existed for a very long time though. Since the monarchy was still in power, I think. At first our economy grew. He encouraged local production for Waerdarei, established trade routes. He won the third political election because of all the good things he'd done, which I understand. But then..." The horses walked side by side and Sparrow tried to relax even though she was still very uncomfortable. "Then one day he fired his entire staff." Fordon lowered her voice excitedly. "Every minister in the entire government, too. He replaced them one by one."

"Oh. But he was allowed right? He is the Chancellor."

"Sure." Fordon patted her horse. "But people were also disappearing. The family of the man who'd won the first political election...one day they were just gone. The Stochhall's disappeared, too. I think they were massacred."

"The Stochhalls?" That name struck a chord inside Sparrow but she couldn't remember from where.

"The old royal family." Fordon sighed. "Who willingly gave up their power to give us democracy only for some evil old dictator to take power over us." She flashed Sparrow a grimace. "And that's when the weirdness started. When he had no one to oppose him, he had the freedom to make any decision he wanted. He closed all public schools, and instead, made it so that only specific schools are open for the few elect. Only people meeting certain requirements are allowed to hold positions of power or free from scrutiny. He runs quite the propaganda machine too, about the Stochhalls or about the old Waerdarei."

"But why is he so evil?" Sparrow didn't get it. "What does he want?"

"Power?" Fordon shrugged. "I think he meant well from the beginning, and yes, I know that is an unpopular opinion. He banned public schools and instead opened Ameliorate Institutes. I'm sure you've heard about them. When it comes to economic growth he is a genius." She lowered her voice. "His biggest mistake was issuing the order against misbehavior." She took a deep breath. "You weren't allowed to express a different opinion. You weren't allowed to talk bad about him or his party, the PFJ."

"What happened if you did?"

"Prison if you were lucky." Fordon snorted. "But society was changing. Human life meant nothing. People were categorized and labeled according to what they could do for others and if you couldn't do anything you'd be discarded. Food became scarce after the Chancellor raided the countryside, massacring our most precious work force. But he only did that during the last 10 years. For the first 20 odd years, Waerdarei blossomed."

"But why?" Sparrow didn't know how she'd missed all of this.

"Who knows." They turned off the main road. "Since food was scarce, people were more desperate. And a desperate man will do a lot to feed himself and his family." She looked over and grinned. "But then he made his second worst mistake. He decided to ban religion. Part of the order against misbehavior, I reckon. People wouldn't believe in him if they believed in God or some rubbish like that. He raided every church and convent from here to the Tall Mountains in the north. He burned almost every house of worship to the ground."

Sparrow shuddered. She didn't think she was religious but she didn't like the idea of churches burning to the ground.

"Why was that his second biggest mistake?" Sparrow needed help connecting the dots.

Fordon looked back at her, grinning so wide her teeth shown.

"Because he found something else in the flames of the churches. He found an adversary. His enemy."

I was raised in a convent, Astrid had said. *I was raised by nuns.*

"General Dace," Sparrow whispered.

"Damn right." Fordon nodded. "General Dace was raised in a church, among holy people. The Chancellor killed everything and everyone she'd ever known and loved. The least she can do is pay him back."

"Oh." Sparrow had more questions than she started with. At least now she knew she didn't side with the Chancellor. She could never. Though she still needed more information on the T.A.L.W. before she could claim total allegiance. She was allowed to have her own opinion, right?

She was about to ask more when Fordon lifted her hand and pointed.

"There! There's Nana's house, come on." She probably forgot that Sparrow had never ridden before because she kicked her horse into a trot.

Sparrow's horse didn't want to be left behind in the dust and started trotting, too. Sparrow's world became bouncy and she grabbed the horn again, almost falling off. She held on for dear life as they got closer to a small cottage sitting on the mountain wall. It might as well have been a part of the mountain if it wasn't for the door and the windows, and the young girl followed by an old woman running down the steps.

Fordon had already gotten off her horse, threw Sparrow's bag on the ground, and lifted the girl up in her arms. Sparrow's horse had stopped still and pulled on the reins to get to the juicy strands of grass that grew there. Fordon's horse was already munching.

Sparrow looked down the side. Had the horse been this tall the entire time? Could she survive jumping down on her own? She let go of the reins, put her leg on the side, and slid down enough so that she was lying on her stomach on the saddle. She was about to slide down the horse when two gentle hands were placed on her hips and Fordon caught her.

"Sorry," Fordon mumbled. Their bodies aligned as Sparrow dropped to the ground, her breasts nestled against Fordon's breastplate. *Was she blushing?* Sparrow almost giggled.

The magic disappeared. Fordon turned around and waved at the old woman and the girl.

"This is Sparrow," she said. "Sparrow, this is my nana."

Nana? Her grandmother. The woman had a full head of white hair and was a few inches shorter than Sparrow. She had the same dimples as Fordon when she smiled.

"Very nice to meet you, Sparrow." She said. "I'm so happy and grateful for everything you're doing at the T.A.L.W."

"Umm, you're welcome." Sparrow raised her eyebrows at Fordon when she was pulled into a bony hug of hard angles.

"I'm Bianca," the girl said. She stepped forward and held out her hand for Sparrow to shake it. "Nice to meet you."

"Bianca is going to come with you," Fordon said. "Any reputable lady needs her own chambermaid."

As much as Fordon and her nana shared the same easy disposition, Bianca looked serious. She had long hair that flowed freely down her shoulders. Not curly, not straight, not wavy. Her eyebrows were dark and her eyelashes thick. She had the same golden eyes that Fordon and their nana had with one big difference. Bianca looked like she'd never smiled once in her life.

"Come on now," Nana said. "Bring the horses to your grandfather in the stable. He put down fresh hay when he heard you were coming." She turned to Sparrow. "Take your bag and come inside. We need to turn you into a lady."

*

Sparrow looked at the cup of swirling liquid placed in front of her. It looked so much thicker than the coffee-replacement she was used to from the House.

"It's coffee." Bianca sipped on her own mug. *Isn't she too young for caffeine?*

They were sitting on a sofa in the main room. Lovely smells came from the kitchen reminding Sparrow that she hadn't had breakfast. Nana was in the kitchen. Bianca and Sparrow were left alone. Fordon still hadn't showed up, she was probably tending to the horses.

Bianca was silent, staring at Sparrow. Her gaze was unnerving. Sparrow wondered what the girl was thinking.

"We're only half-sisters, if you're wondering." Bianca's tone was sharp.

"Oh I wasn't—" Sparrow didn't have time to finish.
"I'm only barely related to Brenna you know."

"Brenna?"

Bianca nodded her head impatiently. "Brenna Fordon, the woman who brought you here, remember her?"

"I don't care who is related to who." Sparrow stared down at the small girl.

"I'm getting to the part which you will care about." Bianca leaned in, talking rapidly. "My father was a very important man to the Chancellor. Our mother was his concubine; Brenna was his slave. They made me." Bianca's eyes shone like lightning. Sparrow could only listen; clearly Bianca wanted to tell her this. "They didn't have to take me in. My father killed Nana's son, Brenna's father. He strung him up by his entrails."

Sparrow leaned back. She wasn't sure she wanted to hear this and she was sure that a girl this young shouldn't have been talking about it.

"Nana wouldn't have taken me in, raised me, fed me, and held me when I was ill if she wasn't the most kind-hearted woman that has ever walked this earth." *Oh.* "If you screw this up in any way by leading danger to this doorstep, *I* will be the one to string *you* up by *your* entrails."

"Stop talking nonsense, Bianca." Nana came into the room with a tray. Accompanying her was a cloud of something spicy with earthy undertones. It smelled like oil. Sparrow's mouth watered. "You'll wind up making her uncomfortable and we don't want her uncomfortable when she goes into the belly of the beast, do we?"

"No, Nana." Bianca took a big sip from her cup. Her gaze never left Sparrow.

The thought that Bianca was going to come with her to AngelGarden was an uncomfortable thought. *If she stares at me like that the entire time, I'm going to go insane.*

"Here you go." Nana handed her a plate completely covered in eggs, fried potatoes, fried ham, sausages, and a red vegetable that Sparrow didn't recognize.

"Thank you so much!" Sparrow's eyes watered as she grabbed the fork and dug in. *I can't believe I'm about to cry at the sight of food.* She ate faster, fully ignoring Bianca's gaze now. She thought the coffee tasted good, but it was nothing compared to this plate of food.

"You city folk from the capital," Nana said. "You eat like animals you do."

Sparrow felt her ears turn pink. She forced herself to slow down.

"No, no," Nana added. "I didn't mean it as an insult. I mean you are starved for real food. There's no fresh food in the city."

"You're right about that." *Stop talking with your mouthful.* Sparrow closed her mouth and smiled sheepishly. She hoped that Nana could at least tell that she appreciated the food. A lot.

Fordon—Brenna—walked in with an old man in tow. They sat down on either side of Bianca, as if trying to keep her safe. Nana handed them plates.

This was family. The intrusive thought filled Sparrow's head. She couldn't remember ever belonging to one. No one had ever kept her safe the way these people clearly loved Bianca. *What was my crime?* Sadness rose within her. She didn't think she'd done anything to deserve what had been given to her. What had happened to all of them?

In that moment, Sparrow found her cause. She found her fight. She didn't know how she would do it. She didn't know if Astrid would help her or if she would have to do it all by herself. But before her death, Sparrow vowed to not rest until every whore house in the entire country was empty.

Chapter Fifteen

A few hours later, Sparrow was grateful to find herself inside a carriage being pulled by the horses rather than riding them. The expensive dress wouldn't have allowed for anything except side-saddle. Bianca was sitting in front of her, wearing a blue dress, a white bolero, and a white hat. She was wearing blush and her disposition was softer but her gaze was just as sharp.

"I almost miss riding." Maybe talking would make it better between them. "Less bumpy." The erratic movement of the carriage was starting to make her feel sick.

Bianca raised one eyebrow but didn't reply. Irritation rose within Sparrow.

"You know when we arrive at AngelGarden," Sparrow said. "You can't keep giving me the silent treatment. Not if we're going to pretend that…"

"You don't need to worry about me." Bianca made a grimace. "I could act before I could talk. In fact, I'm probably the least of your concerns."

"Okay." Sparrow could do nothing but trust her.

She looked out of the window. The nature had changed. They were reaching higher altitudes. The trees were getting sparse and the country was getting harsher. Nothing grew here but orange and yellow flowers. It made the field below look like it was on fire. Sparrow closed her eyes, the world turning inside her head. She didn't know if she was nervous or suffering from motion sickness. She would've given anything to be back in Anchorage, cleaning the bird cages, wishing for Astrid to be near her.

"Do you know the general well?"

"Huh?"

Bianca was looking down at the carriage floor. Sparrow reveled in the small reprieve of not being stared at. "General Dace," Bianca said. "You must mean very much to her for her to give you this honor." She turned her head to the side, still not looking at Sparrow. "What is she like?"

Mean, Sparrow thought. *Teasing. Beautiful. Sad.* "Brave." Sparrow had enough sense to realize that out here, Astrid was more symbol than actual person. "Decisive." She put one arm around her own waist. "I don't think she meant to give me an honor though. I think she just believed I was right for the job."

"And are you?" Bianca looked up again. Something in her eyes reminded Sparrow of the dead fire that burned in Astrid's icy depths. "Right for the job?"

Sparrow surprised herself with her answer. "I am. She must've given it to me for a reason."

A house was getting closer, growing against the horizon. *AngelGarden.* It didn't live up to its name. Sparrow bit her lip until she tasted blood. She hoped that there at least was a garden within those grey walls because outside them, there wasn't. Maybe the chancellor's summer residence was made to instill respect and that's why it stood on a cliff with iron walls all around it. Impenetrable. And very, very ugly.

"I was here once, as a child." Bianca said. "So I know my way around."

Sparrow stared at her. "What if somebody recognizes you?"

"I was five." Bianca lifted her chin. "And I doubt anyone paid attention to Minister Crain's love child."

Crain. The name struck a chord in Sparrow's memory. *An important customer. A painful night.* She looked into Bianca's face, looking for resemblance, not liking what she found. "What happened to your father?"

If Bianca was surprised or upset by the question, she didn't show it. "General Dace killed him." She looked down. "While my mother and I watched."

Sparrow's eyes widened. "What?" Surely, Astrid wouldn't kill a father in front of his family no matter how evil or...

"He led the attack on her convent." Bianca spoke matter-of-factly. "She didn't even notice we were there until she turned around."

Sparrow felt like her heart stand still. "And... and then...?"

The carriage stopped. They were there but Sparrow wasn't ready. She grabbed Bianca's hands to stop her from reaching for the door.

"Bianca, tell me quickly."

Bianca sighed and rolled her eyes.

"My mother made a dash for the general, who knows why. The general shot her right away."

Sparrow startled as if she'd heard the gunshot for real. In her mind's eye she could see Astrid.

"She had this look in her eyes." Bianca's eyes lit up and for a moment they looked alive. "She didn't want to kill my mother, I could tell. When she turned towards me, Brenna came running. To save me. We both wound up joining the T.A.L.W."

Sparrow had more questions. She wanted more time. She also knew that it wasn't Bianca she wanted to ask but General Astrid Dace herself. *Who are you, Astrid?* Who had Sparrow spent the night on the cliff with?

A rapt knocking on the door told Sparrow they had run out of time.

"Thank you for telling me," Sparrow whispered.

"Whatever." Bianca shook her head, looking amused. She opened the door.

Their time had come.

Chapter Sixteen

Sparrow thought she was used to being treated like cattle but a few weeks of freedom had made her used to different standards. She didn't think she was dirty, but Mrs. MacQuoid insisted on bathing her and picking out her underwear and her clothes. Who Mrs. MacQuoid was and why somebody with such a stupid name had anything to say about how Sparrow looked and smelled, Sparrow didn't know. But she didn't complain and neither did Bianca. Bianca, the little weirdo, stood in the corner, holding Sparrow's bag with a sweet smile on her face. Sparrow couldn't help but shoot her a glance or two from the tub.

"Come on, miss," MacQuoid said. "Lean backwards so I can clean you properly."

Sparrow looked up at her. MacQuoid had the blackest eyes she'd ever seen. She'd been scrubbing her back vigorously. What she wanted to do with Sparrow's back was a mystery Sparrow didn't want to solve. She swallowed, wondering if the real Amelie Dartmoor would've allowed this. She leaned back. Mrs. MacQuoid didn't miss a beat now that she had access.

Keep sweet. Just keep sweet. Sparrow gritted her teeth, keeping her face down when a calloused hand touched one of her breasts and then the other. She thought she was going to cry when her hand moved even lower.

"That's enough, if you please." Bianca came to her rescue. "My lady has been traveling all day. Are you sure she isn't clean yet?"

Mrs. MacQuoid pursed her lips and Sparrow could finally breathe when she removed her hand. Before she knew what was happening, she was out of the water and Bianca handed her a towel. Mrs. MacQuoid told her to sit on the bed while she opened a wooden wardrobe, looking at the dresses within.

"We need to choose a proper dress."

"We brought our own clothes." Bianca was still gripping the bag containing the pretty dresses that her nana had packed earlier.

"And you can hang them in the wardrobe later." MacQuoid didn't turn around when she spoke.

Sparrow and Bianca shared a look. All of a sudden, Sparrow was happy that Bianca was there. She was much younger, but she seemed to feel more comfortable here than Sparrow.

"This one will do." The dress that Mrs. MacQuoid took out seemed more expensive than anything Sparrow had ever worn before. It was black and in the kerosene light, it shone as if it was covered in a million small rocks. "We'll need to put your hair up, too."

"I've never worn black before." *It wasn't right.* Black wasn't a color for normal people. It was a color for the people in high society. A color for high born ladies. Not for recovering prostitutes and undercover agents. She swallowed as Mrs. MacQuoid put the dress next to her. She didn't care if it was silly or part of her brain washing or what: Wearing black felt *wrong*.

"Your mother must've worn black, yes?" Without being prompted, MacQuoid started drying her with rough movements, scratching her. *My skin is going to be red.* "I understand that it's hard to go from girl to woman but you are here to…" She cleared her throat. "Well. The

123

Chancellor hopes that you will marry Rufus. And the Chancellor's daughter-in-law, if anyone, can wear black."

Old instincts kicked in. Sparrow looked up at the ceiling as Mrs. MacQuoid dressed her quickly and proficiently. Towel gone. Underwear. Corset. Sparrow closed her eyes, feeling her soul leave her body as she was manhandled. She followed MacQuoid's directions. She didn't listen and didn't notice if MacQuoid complained about the scars on her feet.

She didn't know if it had been minutes or an hour but when she came back to reality, she was dressed, sitting in front of a mirror, and Bianca was tending to her hair. When MacQuoid had left, Sparrow didn't know.

"Welcome back." Bianca's gaze met her in the mirror. It was steady. "Where did you go?"

Sparrow licked her lips, her mouth dry. "Just away." She needed water. She couldn't sound this coarse when meeting the Chancellor and his family.

"I don't envy you." Bianca pulled a brush through her hair one final time and started putting Sparrow's hair up. "I don't envy the experiences that gave you the ability to do that."

"I have a feeling that you have experiences too," Sparrow whispered. "Experiences I don't envy."

Was that a smile? For a moment, Bianca's features softened.

*

Sparrow was standing in the middle of a large room. She looked down at the silk slippers she was wearing. They were black with glittering stones that created flower patterns. The dress was heavy and had many layers around

124

her legs. Bianca had fallen into the background and was standing, head turned down, in line with the other staff. They were waiting for the Chancellor and his wife.

This room lived up to the name of AngelGarden. It had wooden floors and wooden walls. The walls were covered in painted flowers. Not the orange and yellow flowers of the outside, creating the image that the ground was on fire. The flowers of the walls were pale blue, pink, and white. Sparrow didn't think she could ever get bored looking at them. The room had no windows and the fireplace created the belief that it was night-time even though Sparrow knew it was early afternoon.

A door opened at the end of the room. Sparrow instinctively straightened her back, lifted her chin. *Remember, you're a lady. You're wearing black. Act like it.*

Sparrow had never seen the Chancellor in real life. She'd seen photographs of course but nothing could have prepared her for the man that walked in. He had black shaggy hair, a bit of stubble, and his eyes were kinder than she imagined. *This was their enemy?*

"Miss Dartmoor." The hand that shook hers was steadfast and warm. "We're so grateful that you've come."

"Thank you, Chancellor." She tried to curtsy but he stopped her.

"Oh please don't. You're here to be part of the family." He turned to the side. "My wife, Ruby."

Ruby was short, shorter than Sparrow. Her smile mirrored her husband's. Her eyes were green and her hair was dark brown. The only thing that marred the woman's pretty face was a scar that ran down the length of it. Sparrow lowered her gaze, not wanting to be caught staring at the scar.

"Pleased to meet you."

125

"Come now." Ruby put her arm around Sparrow's shoulders. "Walk with me."

She led Sparrow out of the room. Her gait was soft with short steps. A comforting rhythm. The Chancellor fell behind them. A sense of safety enveloped Sparrow. A sense of belonging. She blinked her eyes. This was dangerous. She was in the belly of the beast. It wasn't comforting. It was warm but suffocating. She turned towards Ruby and smiled as sweetly as she could.

They exited the room and walked through a thin corridor. On either side of them, portraits hung. Sparrow glanced at them as they passed. There were various portraits of the Chancellor, sometimes with other people, sometimes alone. As they got further, the portraits got older, showing the Chancellor as a boy with his parents. They reached the end of the corridor and instead of turning left or right and continuing on, they stopped by a window.

"This, dear Amelie." Ruby squeezed her hand. "This is AngelGarden."

Sparrow's mouth dropped open. She'd never seen anything like this. The house looked so metal and barren on the outside. But now, standing here, Sparrow understood the name.

Outside the house, within the walls, a garden grew. Flowerbed after flowerbed, covered in all kinds of flowers, stretched around a stream that began from the top of the garden and disappeared somewhere to the west of the house. There was a barbecue area surrounded by cherry blossom trees. But there was no color. Not a shade of light pink, not even in the cherry blossom. Sparrow didn't know how something so beautiful could look so cold and dead. How did the Chancellor manage to only have white flowers? The stones around the stream were white. Even the stone labs around the barbecue area were white.

"Isn't it beautiful?" Ruby said. "My husband wanted to create a private paradise for our son and me." Her smile was genuine. "My favorite color is white."

White isn't a color, Sparrow wanted to say. *White is the absence of all color.* She buried her feelings and matched Ruby's smile.

"It's so beautiful." She looked back at the garden, the color of bone. "I'd like to take a walk there later." She lowered her gaze. "If I may."

"Of course you can." Ruby looked behind them, probably at the Chancellor. "I'm sure Rufus will take you later. After dinner."

Sparrow looked down at the garden below. She didn't mind letting the Chancellor and his wife think that she admired their garden of skeleton white. It gave her a few moments of reprieve. She tried to focus on her breath, empty her mind. For some reason her mind drifted first to Bianca and then to Astrid. Anchorage felt so far away and yet Sparrow knew that it existed. It was easy to imagine Astrid by the birds. Who would take care of the birds now that Sparrow was away? Somewhere in the back of Sparrow's mind, jealousy arose. Not a strong emotion, still pliant, easily chased away. And yet, it was there. Would Astrid talk to the new bird caretaker, the same way she spoke to Sparrow? Would—

"Come on." The Chancellor spoke. "Let's go to dinner and meet Rufus."

Within a heartbeat, Sparrow turned around, her whimsical thoughts gone. She breathed in deeply, emptying her head until all that was left was the smile playing on her lips. She knew how to greet a customer. This was an act she knew well.

As the Chancellor offered her his arm and she placed her hand on it, feather-light, Sparrow understood why Astrid had chosen her for this assignment. *She knows I'm a prostitute.* Astrid, if anyone, knew what Sparrow had been taught to do. Her body did it for her without a second thought. Smiles. Movements. This was her nature. What she was trained to do.

They walked into the dining hall. By a big fireplace—lit even though it was too warm—stood a young man. He held his head high, as if trying to be taller; however he only reached his father's shoulder. He was an adult, that much was clear, but he had the shoulders of a boy and his smile was kind and shy. In spite of herself, Sparrow felt that she instinctively *liked* him. Not a feeling she'd been expecting.

The Chancellor led her up to Rufus.

"Amelie, this is my son Rufus." There was a chill to the Chancellor's eyes that hadn't been there before. "Rufus, this is Amelie." She could only see the Chancellor from the side, but even from there it looked like he was telling Rufus to *not screw it up.*

Rufus bowed. "Pleased to meet you, Amelie. Welcome to AngelGarden."

Sparrow lowered her head. "Thank you so much. I'm very happy to be here."

Nothing happened. Rufus seemed to want to look anywhere but into Sparrow's eyes. *Should we sit down? Should I say something else?* Sparrow became increasingly aware of the Chancellor's rising annoyance and she wanted to help Rufus. *He is only a boy.*

"I was hoping you would show me the garden afterwards." She had to try. She had to do *something*. "If you don't mind." She turned her face, showing off her best features.

It seemed to work. Rufus's smile was genuine and there was a hint of pink on his cheeks.

"That sounds like a great plan," the Chancellor said. "Why don't you show Amelie to her seat?"

If they'd been back at Madam Crowder's House, Sparrow would've asked the Chancellor to be quiet. To let Rufus talk in his own time. But Sparrow was playing a shy virgin, not an experienced… She held out her hand and placed it on Rufus's arm.

"I'm hungry." She leaned in as close to him as she dared. "I can't wait to see what the Chancellor and his family get to eat." She let the blush rise to her cheeks, playing the role as well as she could. "Sorry." The last word was whispered in Rufus's direction.

"It's okay." Rufus looked relieved. "Since we knew you were coming, I had the cook make father's favorite." His eyes widened as Sparrow moved up next to him. "It's steak." He cleared his throat. "With potatoes and…" He looked flustered. Sparrow was grateful that the Chancellor had returned to his wife's side by the table. If this was going to work, Sparrow and Rufus had to be left alone.

"That sounds delicious," she said in a soft voice. "Where should I sit?"

*

In retrospect, Sparrow didn't know how she pulled it off. She'd gotten used to her freedom. She'd gotten used to not needing to act this way. Not worry about how she looked or how her clothes hung off her. She had to admit that it was a bit fun to be in the inner sanctum. To see how the *other half lived*. To meet the most influential and powerful man of her time. Too bad he was evil.

And too bad he has such a gentle and sensitive son, Sparrow thought. It was after dinner and they were alone in the garden. All the white looked more eerie now that the sun was setting, creating a strange shine that threatened to give Sparrow a headache. Rufus asked her to sit on one of the benches while he pointed out the various white fish that swam in the stream. Sparrow wondered how old he was. Astrid had said he was in his 30s but he looked younger. His eyes held an innocence that she almost found *endearing*. Her heart was starting to hurt over the fact that she was there to betray him, his dad, and their entire kingdom. *Why has he not found a woman yet?* He was an eligible man, son of the Chancellor; surely there should be women knocking down his door asking for a date, nevermind asking to marry him.

"Have you seen these koi fish before?"

It took Sparrow a moment to realize that Rufus had said something that needed a response.

"No, I haven't. At least not white koi." Sparrow hadn't seen any live fish before in her entire life, but she assumed a lady of higher standing would have. "They're beautiful."

"They are." Rufus's smile was full of enthusiasm. "They're my favorite, I think. Most koi have spots of orange and black, but my father managed to procure fish that are only white."

I can see that. Sparrow stifled a yawn. It was getting late and Captain Fordon had woke her up so early…

Rufus sat down next to her. They sat in silence for a bit, watching the water and the fish swim by.

"I know we paid for you to be here." Rufus sighed. "I know my father sent a lot of money to your parents." *Sparrow almost chuckled, wondering what Astrid and the T.A.L.W would spend the money on.* "But I'm very happy you're here."

"Thank you." Sparrow did chuckle then. But it was a soft sound. "I'm happy to be here, too." She straightened her shoulders and let the yawn come. "Oh, excuse me. I've been traveling all day."

"Of course." Rufus stood up so fast it looked like he'd been shot. He offered his arm and Sparrow took it. "You must be tired. You should go to bed right away."

"If I can find my way back to my room." Sparrow looked at the big house in front of them. *And Bianca,* she thought. She was looking forward to seeing the strange girl again, asking how she was, and discussing if either of them had seen any sign of Isabeau. Sparrow hadn't forgotten why she was there.

"When we go inside," Rufus said, "I will call for Mrs. MacQuoid to show you back to your room."

Rufus must have seen her grimace because he nodded in understanding.

"I know," he said. They walked towards the house. The pebbles started to hurt through the thin slippers Sparrow wore. "I know Mrs. MacQuoid isn't the gentlest of creatures but it would be inappropriate for me to follow you to your bedroom. And soon you will know the way there yourself."

Sparrow tried to smile sweetly but the thought of meeting Mrs. MacQuoid again made it difficult. She didn't trust her and part of her wondered what Mrs. MacQuoid

131

had seen when washing her. Surely, you could see signs on Sparrow's body. Signs that she wasn't the virgin lady from high society she was pretending to be.

"You are right," she said and gave his arm a squeeze.

Chapter Seventeen

It was hard to imagine that it had been a week already. A week of monotone walks in the park, stiff dresses, and fatty food she wasn't used to. It seemed as if the family lived the same life every day. Breakfast. Walk in the park. Lunch. Retreat to the study where she was expected to drink tea with the Chancellor's wife. Dinner. Walk in the park. They did everything at the same time every day. And it was *dull*.

This morning, however, a big difference stared Sparrow right in the face at breakfast. The Chancellor was absent. Instead his wife sat at the head of the table. And instead of porridge with cream and sugar, they were offered rolls of bread with ham.

"Thank you." Sparrow wasn't hungry yet, not after the large dinner they had the night before, but she accepted the roll anyway. The one time she refused something offered, Bianca had given her such a talking to. She wasn't about to make the same mistake again.

Rufus gave her a shy smile, before focusing on his own plate. It made Sparrow miss the busy, loud meals in Anchorage.

"The Chancellor..." His wife cleared her throat. "He's been called away. He will be back tomorrow morning."

Rufus nodded, not even looking up from his plate. Something about his stance, however, did change. Sparrow could've sworn she saw tension in his shoulders drop. She looked at him as she bit into her bread. *I understand you,* she thought. *I feel more relaxed too now that you're father's not here.*

The Chancellor's wife cleared her throat again. Sparrow looked up. The crumbs grew in her mouth.

"Have a great day, dears. I'll see you at dinner."

Not at lunch? Sparrow's gaze followed the Chancellor's wife as she got up from the table and left. When she turned her gaze downwards again, she noticed that Rufus was looking at her. His grin was careful.

To her surprise he didn't say anything, but commenced eating his food. Sparrow put down the roll. She didn't want to eat and if no one was watching her, there was no point in forcing it down.

"You will find that the days are different when my father isn't here."

Sparrow met his gaze. The edge of her mouth twitched. "Does that mean we can do whatever we want?"

His cheeks turned slightly pink. Sparrow matched his chuckle. *Gosh, he is cute.* She cringed inwardly. Rufus wasn't cute. He was the son of her enemy. Not cute.

"I want to show you something." His eyes twinkled. He dropped his spoon on the now empty plate. "But I need time to prepare. Can I come and get you in a bit?"

"Yes." She nodded slowly. "Where…. what…?" Was she supposed to just wait in her room?

"Great." He smiled again, showing off the dimple on his left side. "I'll look for you in your room." With that, he left.

Sparrow lowered her hands to her knees. She was alone. The servants hadn't come back to clean the room yet. *Isabeau!* Sparrow didn't want to waste anymore time. She stood up so fast, she knocked her chair backwards. She lifted it upright and then exited the room.

She still didn't know the way around AngelGarden so if anybody found her wandering down the wrong corridor, she couldn't be blamed. Even though she really knew that her room was down the corridor that started with a portrait of an angel weeping. Instead of turning right, she turned left. Her steps picking up and heart pounding, she reached for a random door. She opened it, praying that no one would be on the other side and went through.

She found another corridor with more doors on each side. Sparrow knitted her eyebrows. Seeing no reason to delay, she walked up to the closest door and inspected the handle. It was covered by a fine layer of dust.

"Here I go," she whispered to herself and pulled the door open.

Cold air fell against her, making her shiver in her flimsy dress. It was just another corridor. Sparrow sighed. *Was AngelGarden a maze?* This was getting ridiculous.

At least there were just doors on one side of the corridor now. She chose one at random and pulled it open, no longer careful. Another corridor. Narrower than the others. The door slammed shut behind her.

The air was stale, as if no air had circulated for years. The light on the ceiling flickered. Sparrow took a deep breath. She couldn't panic. Not here. She walked a few steps forward and inspected the doors on both sides.

I'm here to search for Isabeau, she told herself, cursing her own cowardice. Surely Isabeau was meeting a more horrifying danger than stale air and empty corridors.

The floor was cold. So cold that she could feel it through her moccasins. She touched her hand to another door knob. She was no longer as eager to continue. She glanced backwards at the five doors on the other side.

Her heart skipped a beat and her eyes widened. *One, two, three, four, five.* Five doors. She couldn't remember which one she'd come through. She took a step back and looked at the doors on the side she was facing. There were six. *Maybe she had come from that side?* She stood in the middle, moving her head from side to side. Looking through the doors wouldn't help. All there was on the other side was more corridors and more doors. She'd have to open many doors before finding her way back.

"Help," she whimpered. *Why, oh why, had she decided looking around like this was the best choice?* She should've waited for Bianca. She should've made a marking or left crumbs or a thread so she could find her way back. But how was she supposed to know that AngelGarden contained such a maze?

The light flickered again, making a metallic noise. The air felt thicker in her lungs. It felt as if she was drowning and she no longer knew which way was up or which way was down. Her heart beat fast now and she threw herself towards one of the walls, wanting to find something solid behind her back. She was just inside a house. A big house, but a house nonetheless. If she just came up with a strategy, surely she'd make her way out of the maze. Like if she always took the first door in the opposite corner.

Having decided, Sparrow went up to the first door in the opposite corner and opened it. The other side was dark and a strange smell lingered in the air. Sparrow didn't let go of the door and instead squinted, trying to make sense of the room before fully going inside. As her eyes adjusted, she could see that it wasn't a corridor exactly, but a room. There was however, a door on every side of the room—still a part of the maze. Sparrow tried to make sense of what was in the middle. It looked like a sofa and a pile of pillows and blankets. She kept one hand on the door as she walked just a step further, trying to see what it was, her curiosity getting the best of her.

"Amelie!" A firm arm closed around her waist and pulled her back into the corridor.

Sparrow turned around. It was Rufus, looking just as scared as she was.

"What are you doing?" He kept his hand on her shoulder, a comforting touch.

"I got lost." Sparrow didn't need to fake her emotional tumult. "I must've taken a wrong turn from the breakfast nook and then I just lost my way."

Rufus took a deep breath. "Come on, let's get out of here."

He chose one of the doors without difficulty, again and again, until they were back in the original corridor with the painting of the weeping angel.

"How did you know which doors to choose?" Sparrow had to ask.

"The doors leading through or out of the maze have chipped bronze on the door handles. It ends in a man sized vent near the kitchen entrance. It's not even locked. There isn't any need." He grinned.

Oh. But Sparrow still didn't understand something. "But how did you find me?"

"I looked for you in your room," Rufus said. "When I didn't find you there, I knew you must've been lost in the maze. After all, most doors in AngelGarden lead to the maze. Luckily, it's been a while since we were attacked. I just looked at which handles didn't have any dust on them."

"That's smart." Much smarter than Sparrow had expected from Rufus. "But why is there a maze? Inside AngelGarden?"

Rufus led them past Sparrow's sleeping quarters and past the room where they had dinner the previous night. They were now heading up a flight of stairs.

"It's our best defense," Rufus said. "Sure we have walls and an army, but my father didn't think that was enough. He's always said that the best defense comes from within. Should people manage to break down our walls or get inside AngelGarden, they'll never be able to leave. I'm glad I found you when I did." He chuckled, a strange reaction to the current topic. "Father has never even removed the bodies of the people who got lost in there during the last attack."

Sparrow shivered even though she didn't feel cold. She remembered the last room. The dark. The *pillows and blankets*. Maybe it hadn't actually been a pile of pillows but rather the remnants of people who'd gotten lost in the Garden of Angels. She shivered again. What kind of place had Astrid sent her to?

"I know what you're thinking." Rufus met her gaze. They'd almost reached the top of the stairs now.

"What?"

He stopped by a single door that the stairs had led them to. The walls were narrower here which gave an impression that they were at the top of a tower.

"You're wondering how our servants get around." He smiled and it looked like he was about to touch her again. For some reason his smile didn't look as cute now. For a moment, he looked just like his father. "The servants don't know the way around the maze of course, but they know what doors *not* to step through. That means that if they ever rose against us, we could use the maze to escape them. It's ingenious."

Sparrow wasn't sure that she agreed with *ingenious* but she nodded and hoped her smile looked genuine. She didn't know how the Chancellor and his family could live door to door to a deadly maze where its victims still lie. It was vile.

"But forget about the maze now, dear Amelie." Rufus touched his fingers to her hand to get her attention. "I want to show you something else. Something that's all mine."

He opened the door.

Sparrow had been right. They had been in a tower, sort of. What lay in front of them was the roof of AngelGarden. But instead of tiles or rocks, there was a sort of garden there. Potted plants carrying fruits and berries. A wooden hammock built in cherry wood stood in the middle of it all, swaying gently in the wind. Next to it there was a small bookshelf with glass doors filled with various books. And in the distance, the country spread out. Fields and forests and mountains. Things she wasn't able to see from the windows or the garden.

"The garden is my mother's," Rufus said. "The maze is my father's. This is all mine."

Sparrow's mouth fell open in a smile and she stepped carefully. She could feel Rufus's gaze on her but it didn't matter. Her reaction was genuine.

"This is wonderful," she said. "This is the best part of AngelGarden." She turned to look at him. "Thank you for sharing it with me."

"Oh, it's okay." He looked down, his smile a bit sheepish. "My father doesn't even know that I made this; that's why I was hesitant to show you. But he isn't here now and you are and...." He looked up again. His cute smile was back.

"I won't tell anyone."

Sparrow walked over to the edge of the roof and looked at the view. She'd been alive for 27 years and yet she'd never known the world to be so beautiful. She wiped a tear that snuck its way down the side of her cheek. "It's so beautiful." It felt good to speak the truth. To not hold back.

"Right?" Rufus came to stand next to her. "I love coming up here. Good weather, bad weather, doesn't matter. It's a good place to think. And after getting some of my books up here, I spend even more time here." He sighed. "Not when my father is home though." He looked at her. "It's not that he wouldn't approve, of course. Or, I'm not sure actually. I haven't asked." His cheeks turned slightly pink and his hair whipped in the wind. "He has so many plans for me. Every day. I don't get many breaks. Especially since the attack on the capital."

Sparrow's pupils widened and her heart skipped a beat as she remembered that night. The night of terror and blood and screams and death. But it was also the day she got her freedom. She bit her tongue, resisting the wish to ask Rufus about it. *Some people say that the Chancellor was behind the attacks himself. Is that true?*

Rufus chuckled. "At least I can share this with you now." He reached out, took her hand in his, and intertwined their fingers. To Sparrow's surprise it didn't feel as repulsive as it should have.

Chapter Eighteen

They were back at the House in one of the best rooms. The fire created big shadows that danced on the walls. Sparrow couldn't remember ever feeling so comfortable, leaning her head against Astrid's shoulder. Part of her knew that it was a dream; Astrid had never held her like this. For now, this was enough. She could feel Astrid's heartbeat through her back. She didn't think she'd ever heard something so precious. She longed to turn around and press her hand against the sound, the sensation. She didn't dare to move. She didn't want to break the magic. However, she reached for Astrid's arm and placed it around herself.

"This is nice."

The fire crackled. Astrid stretched underneath her but didn't answer.

"Astrid?"

"Hmmm." Astrid's chest trembled.

"I love—"

A hand on her shoulder woke her up. Sparrow opened her eyes. Bianca was leaning over her, wearing the same neutral expression as always.

"A bell rung not long ago," Bianca said. "I think it means it's almost breakfast. Or that breakfast is over. Or maybe it's dinner. It's hard to know without any windows."

"Ok." Sparrow sat up. Her body hurt as if she'd run a marathon and her heart felt heavy.

"Get up now, will you?" Bianca snorted impatiently. "I've already been up for hours. I'm hungry. I can't exactly go and ask for breakfast before my mistress has woken up."

"Fine." Sparrow rubbed her eyes with her knuckles and put her feet on the side of the bed. The marble floor was cold on the soles of her feet. How rich people preferred it to wood or dirt was beyond her.

She walked over to the basin and looked at her face in the mirror. She missed Anchorage. She missed sleeping in a tent. It didn't matter that it was only Bianca and her in the room; it felt like they were being watched. By whom she didn't know.

She dressed quickly, choosing one of the dresses she'd gotten from Fordon's grandmother. It wasn't black but the darkest of greens. The fabric was smooth between her fingers.

"Here." Bianca gestured for Sparrow to put her hair up. She hung a small gold chain around her neck.

"Thanks." Sparrow's mouth was dry. Why did the air feel thick?

"Stop thinking." Bianca squeezed her shoulder. "Go to your happy place. You can do this."

Sparrow nodded. She didn't know why she felt so anxious. This was just a role she needed to play. And even though she was starting to thoroughly enjoy Rufus's company, being at AngelGarden was terrifying. Especially after finding out about the maze.

*

The Chancellor was back today. He sat at the head of the table, wearing the biggest smile on his face. It seemed as if his clothes were brand new, too. His wife sat by his side, looking up at him with admiration in her gaze. Rufus was the only one that acknowledged when Sparrow entered and jumped up from his seat to pull out her chair so she could sit down. It seemed as if their escape to the roof yesterday had made them closer than ever.

"Father came home with some rather good news last night." He sounded a bit breathless as if he couldn't contain his excitement. "His soldiers—"

"Rufus, my boy," the Chancellor interrupted. "Are you really going to deprive me the joy of telling our guest about my biggest triumph?"

Sparrow alternated looking between Rufus and the Chancellor. The Chancellor wasn't smiling, she decided. He was grinning cruelly. Time seemed to slow down and her mouth dried up. When the Chancellor spoke, Sparrow already knew what he was going to say. There was a ringing in her ear. A ringing that sounded like whistling bombs. Falling. Falling. Hitting.

"We found and bombed the rebellion base." The Chancellor's eyes twinkled. "Anchorage or whatever the stupid name was. I was there myself yesterday to inspect it. There's nothing left." He chuckled. "No survivors."

The world stopped. No survivors. Sparrow felt her chest constrict. As if she was buried underneath the rubble. Like she'd died in the House with the others. She wanted to know how it felt when the ashes covered her body, her face, her nose, her mouth. No air.

The sound of her cup meeting the marble floor woke her up. Her hands were shaking and if she hadn't been sitting down she would've fallen. She hadn't known that it was possible to feel like she was dying while still fully alive. Her heart was still pumping. Her lungs were still functioning. She felt the others look at her and she knew

143

that if she didn't react appropriately her cover would be blown and she'd be in danger.

This is bigger than me, Sparrow told herself. *Bianca is here too. I can't put her in danger. Astrid and Fordon would never forgive me.*

"I'm sorry." She exhaled slowly. "I'm sensitive when it comes to death." She hoped that her words were enough. She was doing everything she could not to bawl her eyes out. "Are you not worried that…" Her voice broke. "…General Dace will come and bomb AngelGarden?" She couldn't help the tear that ran down her cheek. "Her retaliation will be horrible." She hoped that she was pulling off a sensitive lady. If they questioned her, or pushed her in any way right now, she would break. Into a million pieces.

"Don't worry." Sparrow couldn't see anything but the Chancellor's teeth. "If she comes here, we will be ready."

Sparrow gasped. "Oh." *The Maze.* The air tightened around her neck. The thought of Astrid, Fordon, Bianca, Gwen, or the doctor being lost in there... The never ending corridors, the doors with nothing behind them but death… Before Sparrow knew what was happening, she fainted and her head landed on the table.

*

When Sparrow woke up, she was in her bed, back in her room. Somebody had placed freshly plucked lavender on her nightstand. Before this, Sparrow hadn't even known white lavenders existed. A sob made Sparrow shift her focus from the flowers to the small person sitting on the floor next to the closed door. It was Bianca, eyes closed, head tilted back. Her eyelids looked red and her cheeks were wet.

Sparrow almost opened her mouth, wanting to comfort her, wanting to say that everything would be okay. Something held her back. She closed her eyes, feeling the unshed tears that rested there. *What would happen to them now?* Sparrow didn't know. *Astrid didn't prepare me for this at all.* Sparrow wanted to scream at her own incompetence. She wanted to scream at all of it. Her upbringing. Her life. This assignment. The stupid dictatorship she lived in. Herself.

She closed her eyes. Maybe if she slept, it would all make sense when she woke up.

*

The next time Sparrow woke up, she noticed the flowers had filled the room with a heady scent. Her skin felt cold and clammy.

"Brenna was supposed to call today. Pretend to be your mother. Check in." Bianca was standing up, her expression a closed wall. "I went to ask the other servants if anybody called. No one has."

Brenna? For a moment Sparrow wasn't sure who Bianca was talking about, but then she remembered. Brenna was Fordon's first name. Sparrow had forgotten that Fordon was supposed to call and check in. Had it really been a couple of weeks already?

"You shouldn't go out looking like that." Sparrow didn't recognize her own voice. "They'll see that you're sad."

"Screw you," Bianca bit back. She started sobbing loudly.

"Stop!" Sparrow jumped from the bed and took Bianca into her arms. She held her as gently as she could. "Don't cry so loudly. They'll hear and we'll both be in danger."

Bianca beat her fist against Sparrow's side but then the tension left her body and she hugged her back. Sparrow didn't know how long they stood there, only that it took a long time for Bianca to stop crying. Enough time for Sparrow's back to start hurting. Reality was sinking in. Anchorage gone. Astrid probably dead. Fordon, too. Sparrow and Bianca all alone in enemy territory with no one to come and rescue them.

"I'm sorry for being a mess," Bianca said into Sparrow's shoulder. "We should both wash up. Sooner or later they're going to come for us. We should be happy." She coughed. "After all, the Chancellor just had a huge breakthrough."

"I don't like to think about it either." Sparrow leaned back and cupped Bianca's face in her hand. She knew that Bianca was more than capable most of the time. "We need to pull it together, okay?"

Bianca nodded.

"We will take a bath," Sparrow continued. "And then we will show our face." She looked at the door. Chills ran down her spine. "Out there."

"Okay." Bianca nodded again. She took a deep breath. "I can do this." She met Sparrow's gaze. "We still need to find out about Captain Tilgadd." Her eyes bore into Sparrow's. "We can do this, right?"

"Yes." Sparrow let go of Bianca's face. She would grieve Astrid and the others later. Now she needed to get to work.

Rufus took her to the roof. No one stopped them. For whatever reason, it seemed as if the Chancellor and his wife appreciated that Sparrow was shook up. Sparrow hoped that they believed she was a sensitive damsel who couldn't handle the tales of attacks or death. Even though Sparrow felt safer with Rufus, it hurt that even with him she couldn't relax.

She touched the handle, feeling the wind on the bare skin of her hands and arms. She closed her eyes, taking deep breaths, facing the direction of Anchorage. Facing the direction of a place that Astrid would never leave. *Don't cry. Don't cry. Don't—*

"I'm sorry it upset you so much." Rufus had come up by her side and placed a hand on the small of her back. "I will do anything to make you feel safe, you know that, right?"

"I know." She forced her eyes to widen and her smile to be sweet. *Like me.* She lowered her gaze. *I'm pretty.* It was second nature to her. Rufus's hand became firmer, telling her that she'd succeeded. She leaned towards him.

He took her hand, brought her fingers up to his lips, and kissed them. "Come on, I'm going to show you something." He led her from the roof.

Rufus brought her to a part of the house she'd never been in. They walked past the doors leading into the maze down to the entrance level. He took her past the main entrance and into a small room that contained stairs leading down.

"I'm not actually supposed to show you this." Rufus's eyes sparkled in the dim light and his teeth shone.

147

Sparrow's heart started pounding and she almost forgot about her grief for a moment. Every cell in her body told her that she was on the verge of discovering…something. Something that would help them.

"These are the dungeons." They were in a large room with cages on each side. "We don't have that many prisoners right now because father believes it's more merciful to let them meet death but…well…."

They walked to the end of the room and Rufus unlocked a door with a small key attached to his belt.

"I wasn't even supposed to have a key but I insisted." He chuckled in a way Sparrow didn't recognize. "Sometimes I come down here just to pound on her a little."

"Her?" Sparrow walked around Rufus to get a better look at whatever it was he wanted to show her. "Pound on?"

It took a few minutes for her eyes to adjust. There was a cage—that much was clear—a cage too small enough to stand up in or stretch your legs in. And in the cage—with angry eyes, scar faced and bloodied, torn clothes—sat Isabeau, looking right at her.

Sparrow's head filled with buzzing and Rufus's voice fell into the background.

"That's why you don't have to be scared, sweet Amelie." He touched his hand to her shoulders and she did her best not to recoil. "Even if the dog leader of the opposition came here, we have the triumph card."

"You come here to beat her?" Isabeau looked straight into her eyes and Sparrow begged for neither of them to give up their secret. Her heart bled for the poor woman, once proud but now broken.

"Oh don't think about her," Rufus said. His voice sounded like his father's. "She's trash. Worthless. She should feel lucky that she's kept alive at all."

"Don't...." She swallowed her words in the last second. She forced her gaze away from Isabeau. "Why is she here? This is your holiday home."

"It was my idea actually." Rufus grinned. *Where was the sweet man I've gotten to know?* "Every attack that the leader *Dace* or whatever has been on herself, this pathetic excuse for a Rathmorian has been with her."

"Don't call me that." Isabeau's voice was low, like a snake's. "I'm not a Rathmorian."

Rufus turned towards Isabeau. *To hit her? To spit at her? To hurt her?*

Sparrow grabbed his arm in panic. "Can we go up to the roof again, please?" She leaned towards him, smiling even though inside she was revolted. To her surprise he nodded.

She'd come back later. Isabeau would be free. If not tonight, then soon.

Chapter Nineteen

Sparrow couldn't wait for the night so she could speak to Bianca freely. She was also eager to head back to Isabeau and check on her properly. She couldn't stop thinking about her in the dungeons. Every minute during lunch. Every minute during the walk in the garden of bones. Every minute during the dinner and subsequent brandy and dessert. Did Isabeau recognize her at all? Was she okay? Sparrow couldn't help but wonder if she had any broken bones or even head damage from being.... She looked at Rufus. She couldn't believe she'd ever thought him sweet or different from his parents.

"I'm sorry." She touched his arm. "I'm a bit tired."

He put his hand on top of hers and gave it a squeeze. "Of course."

"Make sure to rest, dear," the Chancellor's wife said. "I'm sure you'll feel better tomorrow."

Sparrow curtsied and the Chancellor smiled and nodded at her. With a fat cigar in his mouth he looked like a father figure now more than ever. *Don't believe the lie.* She gave them a last smile and exited the room as calmly and graciously as she could, only to start running as soon as the door was closed behind her. She knew that she shouldn't run but the energy in her body needed to escape some way. She kept her steps light and relied on the fact that most servants had retired for the night.

Bianca was already in the room, preparing the beds for the night. Sparrow ran into the room and shut the door behind her. She went up to her and grabbed the girl's hands.

"Wha—"

"Isabeau is alive!"

Bianca's mouth fell open. "Captain Tillgadd is here?" It was as if somebody had lit a candle in Bianca's face and for a moment she looked her age. "But then…all isn't lost?"

"Of course it isn't." Sparrow pulled her into a spontaneous hug. "As long as there is life there is hope." She leaned back to look Bianca in the eyes. "We need to leave. Tonight. We need to leave with Isabeau before they kill her."

"Or before they kill us," Bianca said. "It's getting more and more difficult to pretend to be a rich lady's maid."

"So it's decided." Sparrow's heart started racing again. But it was different now. She didn't need anyone to tell her what to do anymore. She could make her own decisions. She was a free agent, a T.A.L.W. agent. She was going to free Captain Tillgadd tonight. Screw Rufus. Hell could take him and his entire family.

"We're going to free Captain Tillgadd and then go to my grandparents," Bianca said. "Maybe Brenna is there, too. I mean, even if she was in Anchorage during the bombing, she could've survived, right?"

Sparrow sighed. "I'm not going to lie, it doesn't sound good, but I'll also tell you that I was in the capital during the night of the bombing. If I came out of that alive, I'm sure your sister could be okay."

"Let's do this." Bianca got up. "We won't be able to bring our bags, so let's just change our clothes."

"We need clothes for Isabeau as well." Sparrow went over to the wardrobe and pulled off her dress. "Her clothes are dirty."

She took out the most durable dress she had and put on double undergarments since it was cold outside during the night. Her bag stood at the bottom of her wardrobe. She reached inside and grabbed Astrid's jacket. She knew that it was a risk to wear it, but she also couldn't leave it behind. Next to her, Bianca had also gotten dressed in a thicker jacket over her dress. They didn't have much that the tall Isabeau could wear, so Sparrow put a coat over her arm. If worst came to worst, she'd let Isabeau wear Astrid's jacket.

"I want to get some water for her, too."

Bianca produced a small flask from inside the wardrobe and filled it with water from the water basin. Isabeau was also probably hungry but that would have to wait. Sparrow hoped that Isabeau could manage until they got to Bianca and Fordon's grandparents.

"We should wait a few hours, right?" Bianca said just as they were heading out the door. "The Chancellor and his family are still up."

"I don't want to wait." Sparrow's hand was resting on the door knob. If she stopped now she would lose her resolve. "There's no reason for them to use the lower stairway or go down to the dungeons."

"Not even in a drunken stupor to beat on Captain Tillgadd?" Bianca chewed on her lip. Sparrow had never seen her look so worried.

"They might, but Bianca..." Sparrow waited until Bianca looked at her. "This is it. This is now. The situation will never be better. We will never be safe here. We have to do it now. Who knows how things will be a few hours from now."

Bianca took a deep breath, but then she nodded. The flask was still in her hand.

"If we're discovered, we run, okay?" They didn't have any weapons and even if they had, Sparrow didn't think that either of them could fight even one single guard alone.

"Let's go."

They opened the door and snuck out, Sparrow in front since she knew the way. They were about to turn the corner when heavy steps came towards them.

NO! Sparrow turned around, pressing herself and Bianca against the wall. If the guard turned towards them now, the jig was up. *What should I say? What reason would we give?* Sparrow held her breath as the guard turned right and not left, giving them his back. There was still a chance he'd turn around, but Sparrow pulled on Bianca's hand.

She guided Bianca down the stairs, thanking her lucky star that the stairs were made of metal and not wood that could creak. Occasionally they heard voices or footsteps but they didn't meet anymore guards on the way down.

"This way," she whispered, and went down the last set of stairs, heading to the dungeons. She couldn't believe that it'd been that easy. AngelGarden was completely quiet. They hadn't run into anyone from the family or any guard or any—

"It's in here." Sparrow wrapped her fingers around the door knob and twisted. Her heart beat fast from the excitement.

Nothing happened.

She tried again.

"What's happening?" Bianca whispered.

Fuck. "It's locked." Sparrow couldn't believe she'd been so stupid. Had she actually forgotten the whole spiel about Rufus needing a key? And being proud of the fact that he had to *convince* the Chancellor to give him one?

"I'm so stupid," Sparrow hissed at herself. She turned to look at Bianca. "We can't get through the door. We need a key."

"A key?" Bianca pushed Sparrow aside and looked at the lock. "You couldn't have remembered this earlier? Say, before we left the safety of our room?"

"I'm sorry, okay?" Sparrow's chest felt heavy. "What should we do?" Even as she asked the question she knew the answer. Rufus had one.

"We need the key," Bianca said through gritted teeth. She raised her fist as if to hit the door but Sparrow stopped her.

"Don't," she said. "I'll fix it. Just…wait here."

"Wait here?" Bianca's eyes widened. "You want me to wait here."

"Everyone is asleep anyway." Sparrow touched her shoulder. "I'll be back within an hour or earlier. With the key." She didn't want to add the loaded 'if I'm not back by dawn…' and instead gave Bianca what she hoped was a reassuring smile and turned away from the door. She took off her extra clothes and Astrid's jacket, placed them in a pile next to Bianca, and headed back up the stairs.

Her heart grew heavy with each step. She knew what she had to do. It was a dance she had danced many times. She only hoped that Rufus would take the bait.

*

Outside Rufus's bedroom, she bit her lips and pinched her cheeks to create blush and make her lips redder. She pulled her dress to the side to show off her shoulder a bit. She couldn't tell what her hair looked like but it didn't matter. Most men didn't care that much about hair.

"Who's there?"

Sparrow's heart dropped. She turned around, coming face to face with a guard. For a moment fear gripped her throat. The guard's eyes were small, unnaturally pale, like uncooked dough. It felt like he stared into her soul. *Was this an Amelioratite?*

"I'm Amelie." She looked down on the floor, playing coy. "I was…asked for."

The guard had been holding his weapon with one hand but now let it drop to the side. His smile made her insides churn.

"Of course, miss." He nodded and then turned.

She took a deep breath and placed a small smile on her lips. It was time. She needed to focus on this and worry about the guard later. She opened the door and went inside.

"Amelie?" Rufus was sitting on his bed, holding a big book. The room was large with thick curtains hanging over the windows. In the corner, a large wooden desk stood covered with knick-knacks and various books. The main light was off and a small kerosene lamp burned on the nightstand. Next to the lamp, Rufus's key chain lay glistening in the light.

"Rufus." Sparrow took a few steps towards him. She kept her gaze on the floor. "I'm sorry for barging in like this." Her tone was sweet. "I'm having trouble sleeping."

"Oh." He put his book on the side table and got up. He stopped in front of her. "Should I ask Mrs. MacQuoid to send up some warm milk?"

In spite of the situation, Sparrow almost chuckled. "No." She looked up at him. "I was hoping, I mean, I…"

She bit her lip. "I was wondering if I could stay here with you for a little bit."

Rufus produced a sharp intake of breath. "Here?" He sounded immediately out of breath. "With me?" He took another step towards her. "Are you sure that's wise?"

"I can leave before morning." Sparrow met his gaze calmly. *He is so young.* She almost felt bad taking advantage of him…until she remembered poor Isabeau still in the dungeons.

"I don't know what to say."

"So don't say anything." Sparrow made a giggle before she walked up to him and pressed her lips against his. Sickness spread through her stomach as if she'd eaten a bad meal. She put her arms around him. This was something she'd done thousands of times but she'd never hated it this much. She closed her eyes. His lips were dry. *Astrid.* She opened her mouth, letting him kiss her deeper. *Astrid changed everything.*

"Oh." Rufus had started to tremble. He pulled back. "I'm so, so happy you came to AngelGarden."

"Me too." There was no more time to waste. She licked the side of his lip and pushed him backwards until his legs hit the bed. She pushed all thoughts of Astrid to the furthest part of her mind.

To Arms, Liberate Waerdarei.
For Waerdarei. I can do this.

Chapter Twenty

As they lie in the dark, his arm over her chest, she couldn't help but let her mind wander. She wouldn't be able to do her job anymore; that much was clear. *The whole thing was disgusting.* The thought of going back to work as a prostitute was absolutely revolting. And it wasn't just because she'd rather be with Astrid over anyone else. It was also because Sparrow was another person now. She cared for herself and had set standards.

Rufus's breathing was evening out and Sparrow moved his arm as softly as she could, begging that he wouldn't wake up. She looked at his rustled bed hair and round cheeks. She didn't feel anything towards him and the cautious affection she felt a few days ago was completely gone. *I will never sleep with anyone I don't want to again.* It was decided. It didn't matter if Sparrow wound up in the same situation again. This was the last time.

She got up slowly, grabbed the keys, and fled for the door. She didn't know how long she'd been and hoped that Bianca was still by the dungeon door, that nothing had happened. In the corridor, the lights were now off. Sparrow snuck down the corridor, trying to hide in the shadows. She passed by the guard who she spoke to before. He was leaning against the wall, loud snores making the air around him vibrate. Sparrow almost chuckled.

The rest of the house was silent and nothing stopped her on the way down to Bianca.

The girl was sleeping, sitting on their pile of clothes.

"Bianca," Sparrow leaned down and shook her carefully.

"What's happening? Wha— Oh." Bianca opened her eyes. "There you are."

Sparrow lent her a hand and pulled her up.

"You were gone forever." Bianca sounded sleepy and rubbed her face with her hands. "What did you do?"

"It doesn't matter." Sparrow shivered and picked up Astrid's jacket to put it on. "I have the key now." Before Bianca answered, Sparrow put the key in the lock and opened the door.

The room was pitch-black and it took a while for Sparrow's eyes to adjust. Bianca whimpered behind her and she reached back to grab her hand. She could see the grey bars of the cage now and tugged Bianca forward. "Come on."

She walked up to the cage, kneeled, and pulled Bianca down.

"Captain Tillgadd?" Bianca sounded even younger in the dark. "Are you there?"

A grunt came from inside the cage.

"Isabeau. Isabeau, the T.A.L.W. has come to rescue you." Sparrow spoke in a hushed tone even though she wanted to shout. "My name is Sparrow. This is Bianca."

"I'm Captain Fordon's little sister," Bianca said.

Silence fell between them. Sparrow almost gave up when a raspy voice asked, "Do you have any water?"

"Yes!" Bianca held up the flask. "Follow my voice."

You could hear from her grunts and whimpers that Isabeau was in a lot of pain as she dragged herself towards them. She stuck her hand through the bars and Bianca placed the flask in her hand. Isabeau made loud gulps as she drank.

"How hurt are you?" Sparrow was starting to worry.

"I think my legs are fine but one of my arms is broken," Isabeau said when she finished drinking. "And it hurts to breathe. I think I'll be okay if I see a doctor."

"You can walk, right?" Bianca asked.

Isabeau coughed. "If you can get me out of here, I'll manage to walk."

"Do you think the key will work on this lock, too?" Bianca asked.

"There are three keys on the chain," Sparrow said. "It must be one of them. Isabeau, do you know where the lock is?"

"The door to the cage is on my left," Isabeau said. She coughed again. "I'll search for it."

It was too dark to use only eyesight, but together, Isabeau, Sparrow, and Bianca searched the left side of the cage. Finally, Sparrow felt the metal lock in her hand.

"I found it!" She quickly tried one key after the other until a satisfying click told her that the lock was open. She threw it on the floor and pulled the cage open. "Come here."

"Finally." Isabeau shuffled towards them.

Sparrow could hardly believe it when she felt Isabeau's hand and pulled her to a standing position. She'd managed to get Isabeau free without the help of the real T.A.L.W. *Don't celebrate until you're fully out of AngelGarden.*

Isabeau groaned, waking Sparrow from her thoughts.

"Will you manage?" Bianca came up to their side. She grabbed a hold of the fabric of Sparrow's dress as if she didn't want to lose herself in the dark.

"Of course I will." Isabeau already sounded better. There was strength in her voice that hadn't been there before. "Do do you have any weapons?"

"We're hoping to escape without a fight," Sparrow said. They started for the door.

"We have to kill the Chancellor." There was a hard edge in Isabeau's voice. "Or at least his wife or his son. We can't just leave this opportunity."

"This is an opportunity to get out of here alive." Sparrow understood Isabeau. "We need to get out of here. Staying alive is the main objective. I was almost discovered by a guard when getting you out."

"We can't return to General Dace without having done *something.*" They reached the end of the room and Sparrow made sure to lock the door. The longer it took them to find out that they escaped the better.

"Trust me," Bianca chimed in. "General Dace would definitely like us to stay alive more than anything." Bianca and Sparrow looked at each other. They both seemingly agreed that Isabeau didn't need to know the truth yet. She didn't know that it was possible the three of them were the only ones left of the T.A.L.W.

They made their way up the stairs very slowly. It felt as if it took forever. Sparrow counted every breath. All it took was one guard out of bed, or anyone to hear them, and all would be lost. Now she just hoped that the front door didn't have any kind of alarm on it when it opened.

"The door is loud," Bianca said as if reading Sparrow's thoughts. "When we open it, it's going to make a noise."

"So we open it and run like hell." Sparrow's stomach lurched. She didn't know if any of them were up for this. Isabeau was moving so slowly.

Bianca walked ahead of them a few paces, turned the lock on the big door, and opened it. The door made a big groan and cold air washed over them.

"Freedom," Isabeau whispered next to Sparrow.

"I know where the stables are," Bianca whispered. "Come on."

It was dark outside, but the moon shined bright and illuminated their path as they walked across the yard. If they hadn't been in danger, Sparrow would've thought the sight was beautiful. The stable wasn't far away. They'd almost reached it when Isabeau collapsed into Sparrow's arms. She was heavier and bigger and Sparrow almost fell. "Umf."

"What happened?" Bianca came up to them. "She isn't dead is she?"

"No of course not," Sparrow said, but she wasn't sure. "Can you get two horses for us?"

Bianca disappeared into the stable.

Don't fall, don't fall, don't fall. Sparrow's back and arms hurt but she managed to stay up, trying to hold the fallen warrior. She saw Astrid's face in her mind's eye. *I did what you wanted me to do.* Sparrow couldn't help but feel proud.

Bianca came out with two horses, both of them with bare backs. "I'm too short to saddle them," she said. "I hope you don't mind. I know it's not as comfortable—"

"Let's just get out of here. What should we do with her?"

Bianca looked at Isabeau for a long time.

"Hang on." She went back into the stable and came back with a little stool. "I'll stand on the left side of the horse and pull; you stay on the right side and push. We'll

161

get her up on the horse and then I'll sit behind her. You'll ride on the other horse."

"Let's try."

It was a struggle, but soon they managed to get Isabeau up on the horse. Sparrow helped Bianca up behind Isabeau and then got her own horse tied up next to the stable.

"Please be nice to me," she whispered, hoping the horse somehow heard and understood her.

She made eye contact with Bianca and nodded. Isabeau hung forward and Bianca's arms strained visibly, struggling to keep her upright.

I should be the one holding Isabeau, Sparrow thought, *if only I had better balance on a horse.*

They didn't start to gallop until they were far enough away that AngelGarden was just a white shadow behind them. The ride there had seemed so slow and long, but now in the dark, the world rushed by. How the horse didn't lose its footing, Sparrow didn't know. The shadows were long, and all Sparrow could see was the horse in front. She was so tired and tense that she wouldn't have been able to stop the horse even if she wanted to. She just had to trust that Bianca knew where they were going and that neither of them would trip or fall.

When they reached the Fordon residence, it was still night but the horizon was turning pale blue and the world was turning bright. Part of Sparrow still couldn't believe they'd actually managed to escape.

The house looked like last time, peeking out of the mountain like a curious cat. The porch light was on as if they were expecting them. Sparrow pulled on the reins and then jumped off. She hurried over to Bianca. She stood behind Isabeau and caught her as the captain glided off the horse. Bianca jumped off as well.

"Nana and grandpa must be sleeping." Bianca sounded out of breath. Sparrow had a sudden urge to hug her. However, she couldn't move, not while holding Isabeau, who was completely limp. If it wasn't for her raspy breathing, Sparrow would've thought she was dead. They managed to almost carry her before, but Sparrow was tired now.

"Bianca…" Her legs were shaking. "I… can't…" She landed on her butt as her knees buckled and Isabeau fell on top of her.

"Oh no, Sparrow. Wait here." Bianca left the horses as they were and ran towards the house. The door was locked and as Sparrow looked on from the ground, Bianca started banging on the front door.

"Nana! Open." There were tears in her voice. "Please, please wake up."

Her screams echoed in the night. After days of quiet, careful voices it sounded so unnatural.

"Nana! Grandpa!"

"Bianca," Sparrow called from her place on the ground. "You don't know who can hear you, don't you have a—"

The light inside turned on and the door flung open. Before Bianca had a chance to react, she was swept up in a hug. Sparrow felt tears flow down her cheeks and she cradled Isabeau harder. She cried for Isabeau and for Rufus; she cried for Bianca and the entire Fordon family; she cried for herself and the hand she'd been dealt. Lastly, she cried for Astrid and the lives that had been lost. And all the lives that would be lost before the fight was over.

Chapter Twenty-One

Sparrow was lying on a bed alone. Bianca had disappeared somewhere with her grandparents and Isabeau was placed in another bed with several blankets on top. The sun hung high outside but the thick curtains made the room dark. Sparrow didn't know if she could sleep. It felt strange to be *safe?* She sighed and dug her fingers into the rough sheet. *Am I safe?*

"I still can't believe you made your way out of there. With Captain Tilgadd as well." Fordon was standing in the doorway. She had her arm in a sling and a black eye but she was alive. Sparrow sat up, her tired body complaining.

"You're alive." Her voice croaked.

"Most of us are," Fordon took a few steps into the room. She was limping. "The Chancellor didn't kill nearly as many people as he thinks."

Sparrow swallowed, her mouth dry. *Astrid.* She tried to say her name but she couldn't get it out. *General Dace? Is the general alive?* She couldn't manage that either. She opened and closed her mouth a few times like a fish out of water. Sweat clung to her skin. Was she going to throw up? Was she going to faint again? At least she was in a bed this time. She looked at Fordon with wide eyes, hoping she could understand her question.

Of course she couldn't.

"Anchorage is pretty gone though," Fordon sighed. "General Dace—"

"Yes." Sparrow's heartbeat picked up. "Yes?"

"She's heartbroken."

Sparrow thought she'd start crying again. "She… is… alive?"

"Of course she is," Fordon came and sat down on the end of her bed. She stretched her back with a groan. "When the bombs fell we ran into the forest. They bombed the church first, killing half of the captains." She grimaced from pain. "I was standing in the corridor downstairs and managed to get out just in the nick of time."

Sparrow's mind went to the attic, to all the birds. Imagining them all dead was strange. "And Ast— General Dace? What about her?"

"I don't know how she managed to get out of that." Fordon shook her head. "I really don't. Suddenly she was next to me. We tried to get everyone to run as the bombs started falling."

Did Gwen make it? Sparrow wondered. *Did the doctor? Did any of the children? The nice woman who always made her food?* She pulled Astrid's jacket tighter around her, her fingers clutching at the hem of it.

"Where is General Dace now?"

"At the new camp I think," Fordon said. "It's hidden deep in the forest behind Anchorage. We didn't want to go far, thinking they wouldn't bomb the same place twice."

"Is that really wise?" Sparrow wanted Astrid far away from the danger. She still shuddered at the memory of whistling bombs.

"It's not up to me," Fordon said. "Luckily, I'm not the one responsible for everyone. I couldn't handle it."

"I want to see her." Sparrow stood up and started pulling on the socks of her icy cold feet. She would sleep when this was over. After she saw with her own eyes that Astrid was alive and well. "I want to see her now."

"Wait." Fordon got up and grabbed a hold of Sparrow's arm. "Just wait a second."

Sparrow stopped moving; her body was trembling. "I need to see the general now." Her voice trembled too. "Can I take a horse? Please." Their gazes met. "*Please.*"

"Come on." Fordon guided her back to the bed. Sparrow swallowed back tears. "Right now you need to rest. The general will know that you rescued Captain Tilgadd."

"That's not what I'm worried about." Sparrow struggled against her when Fordon pushed her back towards the bed. "I need to see her. I need to talk to her." She sat up again but didn't try to get off the bed. She stared at Fordon, her chest heaving.

"I've already sent word to the general," Fordon said. "She'll be here by nightfall."

"Nightfall?" Sparrow's eyes grew wide. "Here. Here."

"She needs to speak to Captain Tilgadd and bring her home."

The words cut Sparrow. Was Astrid only coming to see Isabeau? Or was there a part of her that thought about Sparrow at all? "If I go to sleep..." She stared at Fordon. "...will you wake me up before she arrives?"

Fordon agreed and left Sparrow alone. Except for Fordon's steps, the house was silent. It was strange being alone after sleeping in the same room as Bianca for the past couple of weeks. *I wonder where Bianca is.* Had she lay down next to her grandma? Was she in another room somewhere? Sleeping? Awake? Was she watching over Isabeau? No one paid attention to Sparrow except for asking her if she was hurt and showing her to this room.

I've been used. And now she wasn't needed anymore.

*

Sparrow was dreaming of whistling bombs when Fordon came to wake her up.

"She's here." That was all it took for Sparrow's eyes to open.

The curtain had been pulled up and sunlight streamed into the room.

Sparrow pushed Fordon's hand away and sat up.

"I told you to wake me up before she arrived."

"I didn't know she would be this quick," Fordon said. "I was sure she'd wait until nightfall to travel here." She gritted her teeth. "Seems like she couldn't wait."

"I suppose so." Sparrow got up and stretched her back. It felt like she'd run a marathon. In her mind she could see Astrid's face when she saw Isabeau again. The relief at being reunited with her friend. The affection that would shine in those icy blue eyes.

"I need the restroom," she told Fordon. It didn't matter but she needed to look in a mirror before she was ready to meet Astrid. Just in case.

Fordon showed her down a hallway and pointed to a small room at the end of it. There were movements and voices within the house and Sparrow listened carefully. She couldn't hear what the low voices were saying, but her entire body reacted to a tone that had to be Astrid's.

"Thanks," she mumbled to Fordon as she entered the bathroom and closed the door.

The bathroom was the first room that proved the Fordon house really was part of the mountain. One of the

167

walls was made of rock, covered in condensation and some moss. Sparrow went over to the wall and pressed her hands and face against it, grateful for the cold. Grateful for the moment of peace. In a bit she would go out and meet Astrid again. What would happen after—how either of them would react—she didn't know. A spider was making a web between the toilet and the mountain wall. *This is the strangest bathroom I've ever seen.*

She turned around to look at herself in the mirror. She looked a bit plumper than she remembered, having put on necessary weight. Her hair was messy but there wasn't enough time to fix it. She was still wearing the same dress as the night before and Astrid's jacket over it.

"It's time Astrid gets her jacket back."

Chapter Twenty-Two

Astrid was sitting by Isabeau's bed, turned away from the spot where Sparrow had appeared. Bianca and Fordon were standing on the opposite side of the room, Fordon with her arm around Bianca's shoulders.

Isabeau was awake and as soon as Sparrow came into the room, her mouth cracked into a smile as their gazes met.

"There's my savior." She laughed. "I was wondering when you were going to show up."

It felt like time stood still. Astrid turned around. Her mouth fell open. It wasn't a smile but it wasn't far from it. Sparrow couldn't stop looking at those blue eyes.

"It's the rat catcher." Astrid's words made her blush. "Seems like you did catch something bigger."

Sparrow went into the room and sat down on the floor by Isabeau's feet next to Astrid. Instead of doing what she wanted, which was to look at Astrid, hug Astrid, talk to Astrid, she focused on Isabeau, who looked better now even though she was still pale.

"Thank you for getting me here," Isabeau said. "Bianca told me you're the one who found me."

"I couldn't have gotten any of us out without her." Sparrow looked up at Bianca and was greeted with a smile. In spite of their difference in age and experiences, Bianca was someone she would miss like a lost limb. Being stuck in enemy territory had fused them together. She felt Astrid's icy gaze burning into the side of her face.

Eventually she couldn't look away anymore.

"You did better than I'd hoped." There was a bruise on Astrid's right cheek and now that she was closer, Sparrow noticed that there was a tension in her shoulders that hadn't been there before.

"I understand it now." There was so much she wanted to say and she didn't know where to start. "I understand your fight. I understand everything."

Astrid's face lit up.

"I'll keep helping," Sparrow continued. "If you'll have me."

"I'm sure we can find use for you." Astrid cleared her throat and looked back at Isabeau. "At first I have to think of a proper reward for you, for bringing Captain Tillgadd back to us."

Sparrow smiled and looked down at her hands in her lap. Her fingers tensed so hard her knuckles were whitening. She wanted to speak freely with Astrid but knew she couldn't do that here. Instead she asked what she knew was safe to ask. "What do we do now?"

"Captain Tillgadd shall stay here," Astrid said with authority in her voice. "I know you want to come with me." She put a hand to Isabeau's shoulder. "But I need you to be completely well before you join us. The good people here will take care of you. Captain Fordon, I expect you to defend this family and Isabeau with your life." For once she used Isabeau's first name.

"They're my family," Fordon said. "Of course I will."

"And you." Astrid looked at Sparrow again. "You will go back with me to Anchorage, if you want to."

Sparrow nodded. Wherever Astrid went, she would follow. Whether Astrid wanted her to or not.

Saying goodbye to Bianca was harder than Sparrow anticipated. These were uncertain times and it felt strange to think that they might never see each other again.

"You're the bravest person I've ever met," Sparrow told her as they hugged for a long time.

Bianca sighed and leaned back. "I was terrified the entire time."

"Me too." She touched a hand to Bianca's cheek. "Let's be careful to not lose ourselves, yes?"

Bianca nodded.

"Let's go," Astrid called. "The longer time passes since your escape the more dangerous the trail becomes."

Sparrow turned around. Astrid stood next to a white horse with black spots. Probably the same horse that she'd arrived with a few hours earlier. *Was she expecting them to share a horse?*

"It'll be safer on one horse," Astrid said. "Less noise. Less likely we'll be discovered, and should we be chased or found, there's no risk we'll be separated. Come here."

Sparrow flashed Bianca one last smile then turned towards Astrid. Her knees felt gooey.

"Come on." Astrid's eyes flashed impatiently. She looked worried. Maybe she really was worried that someone would snatch them up during their ride to Anchorage. Or perhaps she was feeling like Sparrow, worried about being alone together. How that would feel. It felt as if she was moving in slow motion, as if she was disconnected from her own body.

She held out her hands, letting Sparrow step in them and boosted her up. Then Astrid put her own foot in the stirrups and got up behind Sparrow. Sparrow couldn't help her body's reaction. She sank into Astrid's body as Astrid grabbed the reins with her arms around Sparrow's waist. Astrid's body was otherwise very still, as if she was scared of moving.

"Let's go," she mumbled near Sparrow's ear.

She kicked the horse into a walk, then a trot, then a gallop. Sparrow tried to think of anything else. Of the danger they were in. Of the T.A.L.W. and the fight that was waiting. But all she could think about was Astrid's muscled thighs pressed against her and the firm body keeping her upright. The horse moved in fluid movements with the world rushing by.

Sparrow wished she could've seen Astrid's facial expression. After all, she could've sat behind the saddle, but instead, Astrid wanted her in the front. She wanted Sparrow there. To have her arms around Sparrow? To feel her near? Sparrow could only hope. She could feel Astrid's chin almost resting on her shoulder and it made her throat dry. How she'd manage the entire ride without combusting, she didn't know.

"Oh damn," Astrid swore from behind her.

Sparrow could hear it too. An engine was running somewhere high above them. "Do you think they're looking for us?"

"It doesn't matter if they're looking for us or not," Astrid pulled on the reins, making the horse slow down. "If they find us, who knows what we'll do. Hang on." She turned the horse to the side and they rode into the thick forest. Astrid pulled the horse to a halt, jumped off, and motioned for Sparrow to do the same.

"Hold him." Astrid handed Sparrow the reins and walked towards the road. There were more engines now. Not just above but around them. They sounded close.

"Astrid," Sparrow whispered. "Come back." If Astrid was discovered and taken right in front of her, Sparrow wouldn't know what to do.

"Fuck." Astrid was suddenly beside her again. "It seems like the Chancellor has sent the entire cavalry after you. Probably the Amelioratites, too."

"Oh no." Sparrow's heart jolted. "What should we do?"

"We need to get back to Anchorage. I have a plan I need to share with my captains." She took the reins from Sparrow's hands. "We need to stick to the forest though, under the trees where they can't see us. It'll take us much longer."

Sparrow nodded. "Let's go then."

They started walking together, moving slowly so as to not make much noise. The forest was filled with sounds from birds, cracking leaves and sticks, the wind moving the trees, and underneath it all, engines. After a while, Sparrow realized it wasn't just the noise of engines but also the roar of distant thunder.

"If there's a storm, we'll need to seek shelter," Astrid said, as if reading Sparrow's mind. "There are some caves up ahead. I'm sure we can find something. It's getting dark as well; the forest will be treacherous."

Sparrow couldn't do anything but agree. Even though she'd slept in Fordon's house, she was tired in a way she hadn't been earlier and was longing for proper rest. It felt like all she'd done for days was be on the run.

A loud rumble accompanied by a flash of lightning made both Sparrow and the horse jump. Astrid turned to the horse to soothe it while Sparrow grabbed a hold of Astrid's jacket.

"Calm down, calm down, shhh," Astrid said. Sparrow knew she was talking to the horse, but she closed her eyes and kept close, letting Astrid's voice soothe her, too. Her heart was beating so fast it felt like Astrid would be able to feel it through her back. Sparrow didn't care. If they were going to die right here, right now, it was important Astrid knew that somebody cared for *her*. Not General Dace, not her efforts, just Astrid. For her blue eyes. For her smile. For her voice.

"Come on." Astrid turned around so she could place one arm around Sparrow, and with a firm grip on both Sparrow and the horse, Astrid forced the trio forward. "Let's find a cave."

Before it got completely dark, they found a cave in the mountain. Sparrow sat down against the wall, looking at Astrid with the horse. Astrid took the saddle and bridle off.

"Won't he run away?" Sparrow leaned her head against the stone. She was so tired. Both emotionally and physically.

"No." Astrid put the horse's equipment down next to the wall. "I don't think he'll leave me to run into a storm."

Sparrow looked towards the cave entrance. The rain poured down outside, and from time to time, the thunder rumbled. Inside the cave there was peace.

Astrid came and sat down next to her. Their arms touched. Sparrow took a deep breath, feeling herself relax. The ground was hard underneath them but it didn't matter.

"So how was it, rat ca—" Astrid cleared her throat. "Sparrow." She chuckled. "I'm sorry, I just can't take that name seriously."

"You're so mean." Sparrow bumped their shoulders together. She wasn't actually offended. Astrid could call her anything she liked. She chuckled to show that she wasn't offended.

"How was it?" Astrid took a deep breath. "At AngelGarden?"

"Oh." Sparrow knew this question would come, but after the night with Rufus she wasn't sure what to say. "There's a maze inside," she said. "In case anyone attacks."

"A maze?" Astrid lifted one of her eyebrows.

"Yes." Now that Astrid was looking right at her, Sparrow couldn't look away. She was close enough to count every eyelash, every bump and bruise and scar. Astrid was very beautiful for having so many scars on her face. "There's a maze inside AngelGarden, constructed so that if they're attacked the attackers will die in the middle." Astrid didn't look impressed so Sparrow kept talking. "It's horrible, Astrid. I got lost in it once and there are bodies there. People who got lost. I don't think even I could find my way through it and that's after Rufus explained it to me."

"Was Rufus good to you?" Something flashed in Astrid's eyes.

Doesn't she want to hear more about the maze?

"He was fine." Sparrow closed her eyes. She wanted to forget the feel of his body. "Sweet at times. But I heard him speak about Isabeau; I heard him speak about...speak about you." She shivered and pulled the jacket closer around her. "It hurt me every time they called you a dog."

Astrid's eyes revealed no emotion. Sparrow wanted to hug her. Take her in her arms. Kiss away the tears she wasn't crying.

"You shouldn't care about what they call me." Astrid folded her arms over her chest. Goosebumps stood up on her neck, showing that she was just as cold as Sparrow. "I can't believe I let him bomb Anchorage."

"I'm sure there wasn't anything you could've done," Sparrow said. "You don't have special powers. How were you going to stop bombs from falling?"

"I could've established the T.A.L.W. in a less obvious place." Astrid shook her head and looked at Sparrow. "It was irresponsible of me. I just thought that it was better to hide in the open."

"What was so special about Anchorage?" Something was lurking underneath the surface. "Why did you keep the T.A.L.W there?"

"I was raised here." Astrid made a dismissive gesture with her hand.

"Here?" Sparrow didn't get what she meant. "In the cave?"

"Not in the cave, you idiot."Astrid flicked her on the nose. "At Anchorage. At that church. A convent lived there. Nuns."

A memory formed in Sparrow's mind. Something that Bianca had told her. "Minister Crane slaughtered everyone."

Astrid looked surprised. "You know this?"

"I didn't know that Anchorage was that convent," Sparrow said. "But you told me about growing up in a convent."

"It was 15 years ago." Astrid seemed to bite her lips between words. "I wasn't a child, I was an adult but I loved life in the convent. All I had to do was help with the garden. Otherwise I could spend my days reading and writing stories."

Astrid, careless like this, was hard to explain. Sparrow reached forward and grabbed her hand. She wanted them to be connected while Astrid told her story.

"They came out of nowhere. No bombs because those hadn't been invented yet. But they had guns. Big guns. The nuns—my family—didn't stand a chance. And I ran into the forest, scared. I didn't stay and fight." She held up a hand before Sparrow had a chance to say anything. "There was nothing I could do, I know that. And the Mothers wanted me to save myself, I know that, too. I still have survivor's guilt, but that's natural. And I've avenged them a thousand times over." Her eyes shone.

"Why did they kill everyone?" Sparrow ran her thumb over Astrid's knuckles.

"Religion isn't allowed." Astrid laughed mirthlessly. "I didn't know it at the time, but *he* had issued a degree earlier that year banning all forms of religion. The Mothers at the convent knew but had enough integrity to keep going, living the life they wanted to live."

"What did you do after it had happened?"

Astrid shook her head. "I died. That's what happened. I was also born. I started the T.A.L.W. about seven years ago and like an idiot, I placed our base at the same convent. I made history repeat itself." She wiped away a tear. "For that, there's no forgiveness."

"I forgive you." Sparrow waited until Astrid looked at her. "I forgive you. I forgive you for all the lives lost. I forgive you for placing Bianca and me at AngelGarden. I forgive you for all of it." Astrid's face was a question mark. Sparrow cradled her cheek. "If not me, then who? I am of the people. I was sold as a sex slave. I survived the bombing of the capital. Why can't I give you forgiveness? You are forgiven."

Astrid's facial expression was different, her eyes open, the look in them vulnerable. The curtain pulled away. A woman stared back at Sparrow. A woman freed. For a moment, Sparrow felt loved. She felt adored. And she felt grateful that she'd been able to give anything at all.

Chapter Twenty-Three

It was still early when Astrid shook her shoulders to wake her up. Sparrow's back ached, but her dreams had been nice.

"Why are you smiling?" Astrid asked. "Not that I mind."

"I was dreaming about the Stonehills." Sparrow sat up and rubbed her eyes. "My family."

"You've never mentioned them before."

"I know," Sparrow said. "Because I don't remember them. Not really. I think my mother was beautiful. And there was another figure, a man. Not my father." She closed her eyes, remembering gray hair and a beard, rough against her cheek when they hugged. "An uncle maybe? Or a grandfather." She smiled at Astrid. "It was a nice dream anyway."

Astrid sighed and nodded. It looked like she wasn't sure what to say. Sparrow pushed her hair from her face, wishing for a shower. The dream was fading fast.

They walked through the forest. Sparrow had no idea where they were going and hoped that Astrid knew the way. They—the horse as well—climbed over several fallen trees, and suddenly there was a smell of ash in the air.

"We're getting close," Astrid said. "Just past this hill."

And they were there. Anchorage. Or what was left of it. There were broken tents and huts everywhere. The medicine shack was completely destroyed. The church still smoldered.

"It burnt for days." Astrid looked up at the church.

They started walking through the carnage. There were no bodies but signs of death nonetheless. Piles of bloody, torn clothes. Sparrow wondered if the people of Anchorage really had been that quick to bury them all.

"How did you survive?" She asked Astrid. "I heard you were in the church and that they bombed that first."

"Oh." Astrid stopped where they stood, took off all the tack from the horse and then gave it a smack on the bottom. "He'll find his way," she said to Sparrow's questioning face. "I just got lucky. When the bomb fell I was pushed under the staircase. Most were not so lucky."

"And now you're living in the forest behind the church?"

"Yes. I know it sounds like a mistake but it isn't." Astrid sounded sure. "They believe we'll regroup elsewhere, not that we'll still be here. Hiding." She made a fist. "And he'll never see our attack coming."

Sparrow didn't know how to answer that. She followed Astrid through to the clearing and behind the church. They didn't have to walk long before they encountered tents and fires on the forest floor. There they all were. Familiar faces. Familiar sights.

"It's like coming home." Sparrow hadn't known she said it out loud until Astrid bumped their hips together.

"That's good," she said. "This is my home, too."

Joy filled Sparrow and she tentatively reached for Astrid's hand. She wanted to join them together, bask even more in this feeling of belonging. She didn't care if anyone saw or what they thought.

"Sparrow! Is that you?" A familiar voice made her turn around, away from Astrid. Before she could react, Gwen threw herself at Sparrow with her arms around her neck. "You're alive! I can't believe you're alive and... and... *here!*"

Sparrow tried to hug her back as best she could but was soon bothered by the suffocating embrace. Luckily, Gwen retreated just the moment she couldn't stand it anymore. Sparrow could see that Gwen was badly burnt on the side of her face.

"You're hurt." She reached up, but Gwen took a step back before Sparrow could reach it.

"Hey, it still hurts, no touchy."

Only Gwen can talk that way, Sparrow thought. She turned around to join Astrid in the conversation but the general was gone. Had she really just left without saying so much as a word? After the night in the cave? Sparrow felt goose bumps forming on her back and she shivered. At least she still had Astrid's jacket. A fabric reminder of what might be. She finally spied the general, standing not too far away, speaking with captains.

That's when she noticed that Gwen was still talking.

"...it was so scary but the majority of the people survived. The main deaths were of captains and I'm not saying that's better, I'm just saying that at least they're fine with dying. Well, maybe not *fine* with dying but more fine than poor refugees who fled from death. The good doctor's fine, which was a blessing. Not saying that she's the most important person but without her more people would've died. We're training more people to become doctors." She linked her arm with Sparrow. "Come on, let me show you around."

Sparrow threw a final glance at Astrid who was still talking. Tension was back in her shoulders and she looked like she was angry. Sparrow couldn't go there; it didn't matter how much she wanted to.

"Okay." She nodded. "Show me around."

"Great," Gwen said. "As you can see, it's not as big as the original Anchorage, and there's no church to hold meetings in but it still feels like Anchorage, you know? And it's good enough to regroup." She started guiding Sparrow between the tents. "I want a huge fort for us in the future. A medical wing, a wing for the meetings, rooms for refugees—impenetrable."

"I don't think any fort is impenetrable." Sparrow nodded at some familiar faces. *Not against bombs at least.*

"I suppose not," Gwen continued. "But it feels like we're hiding. I wish we could be out in the open." They stopped in front of an enclosure. Several horses were inside, including the one that had carried Astrid and Sparrow there. "This is where we keep the horses. We don't have a stable but some of the refugees are working on building one. Just so they have shelter. Like the storm last night; they were so nervous. Hey, Stephen!" She waved at a thin, red haired young man that Sparrow hadn't seen before. Maybe he was new.

"I can imagine." Sparrow remembered her own feelings about the loud thunder. Not to mention the horse's reaction. "What are those?" Behind the enclosure there was a big open tent with a cooking area underneath, and next to it, several flimsy shacks were erected. They looked like something a child might build.

"That's the new *church*." Gwen made a gesture towards them with both hands. "Well, it's a place for the captains to have meetings. One of them is the general's sleeping quarters." Sparrow listened intently. "She insisted that she could sleep in tents just like the rest of us. But we insisted that our general needs to sleep in a proper house." Gwen giggled. "Not that that's a proper house. But you know what I mean." She sighed. "Not that General Dace is here much. Since the bombing she seems to never be in Anchorage. She takes long rides or walks. Disappears for days."

"She came to get me," Sparrow said.

"Yes, I understand that," Gwen said. "But what about all the other times?"

Sparrow didn't have an answer.

"So what are the sleeping arrangements like?" She asked instead. "Do I get a tent?"

Gwen made a grimace.

"Not exactly." She walked up to one of the horses and offered an apple she pulled out from her pocket. "There are no free beds here, but you can go back to old Anchorage and see if you find any tents that will work and bring it here. Alternatively, just sleep under the stars for a while."

Sparrow looked up at the sky between the tree tops. It was still cloudy. Gwen seemed to be reading her mind.

"Yeah, I know, it might rain. I'd invite you in to the medical shack with me but we're full of patients."

"I'll manage," Sparrow said. She wanted to be left alone. So many things had happened in the past few days she no longer knew what was up or what was down. She forced a smile. "Thank you for showing me around, Gwen. I think I want to be by myself now."

"I need to get back anyway." Gwen squeezed her shoulder. "Come and find me later, okay? I want to hear all about your adventure."

Sparrow could only stare as Gwen left her by the horses. She wasn't staring at Gwen; her gaze was following Astrid as the general left the group of people she'd been talking to. She walked over to the shack with the green door and went inside. Closing the door felt final. Sparrow was left on the other side.

It doesn't matter what we've shared. Sparrow sighed. *Astrid will always be General Dace. Not my friend. Not my lover.* One of the horses leaned over the fence and pressed his muzzle against Sparrow's cheek. It was silky smooth and his warm breath washed over her, soothing. She lifted up her hand and tugged affectionately at the fringe of the horse.

"Thank you," she told him. "Maybe they'll let me help take care of you." Horses didn't seem half as scary now as they had a week ago. Or maybe she should ask if she could take care of the birds again. If there were still some alive and they hadn't all died. She grinned and scratched the horse's forehead. "Or maybe I could catch rats for them again."

She turned away from the enclosure and looked over New Anchorage. She looked at the people, the trees, and the camp fires. A butterfly fluttered near. *Freedom.* This was freedom. Sparrow smiled at no one and looked up at the sky. The sun was shining through the clouds.

Chapter Twenty-Four

It was night time. Sparrow had spent the day near the horses, not wanting to go anywhere else. The sun had set and Sparrow knew she should have set off for the clearing to find a tent. Instead she found herself loitering outside Astrid's shack. She knew she shouldn't bother her but still she couldn't stay away. Most of the people had gone to sleep now and the camp was quiet. No one would see her. No one would notice her.

Sparrow went up to the door and knocked. No answer. *I know she's in there,* Sparrow thought. She saw her enter after dinner. The door had a simple latch, and before she could stop herself, Sparrow opened it.

"Excuse me, what—oh it's the rat catcher." Astrid was sitting on a bench with her feet on the table. Her boots were off, her naked feet sticking out of her leather trousers. Otherwise she was still wearing her full armor including gloves. She had a wine bottle in her hand which she took a swig from. "Come on, sit down."

Sparrow looked around, but there was nowhere to sit. The shack was small and sparsely furnished. Sparrow didn't think that Astrid wanted her to sit on the floor. Or on the bed. Sparrow's gaze stayed on the bed and she licked her lips, almost by compulsion. She turned around and looked at Astrid again.

"I don't know what I'm doing here."

Astrid lifted her chin up. There was something strange in her gaze, like fog but more lethal. Goose bumps traveled through Sparrow's body.

185

"I do." Astrid got up from the bench and made a gesture. "Sit down." She took the wine with her and sat down on the bed.

"I didn't mean to put you out." Sparrow sank down on the bench.

"It's no problem." Astrid drank from the bottle again. "Want some?"

"No thank you."

They sat in silence for many heart beats. Sparrow didn't know what to say; she just enjoyed being near Astrid. Even if all Astrid was doing was drinking and sometimes sighing. The shack was surprisingly sturdy and even though the rain had started to fall and it was windy outside, it was cozy inside. Or maybe she was just basking in Astrid's presence. There was a map on the table in front of Sparrow and she looked at it with interest. She'd never seen a map of the place where she lived before.

"What am I to you?" The question fell to the ground between them. Astrid put the bottle on the floor and got up from the bed. She went up to Sparrow and looked down at her. "Am I anything at all?"

How can she ask me that? Sparrow didn't know whether to laugh or cry. This was the question she wanted to ask. Sparrow had no way of knowing what Astrid was feeling. She'd been sounding so hollow. A sudden realization made Sparrow stand up. She realized she hadn't answered yet and her mind raced to find a proper answer. She didn't want to say just anything. She wanted to say the right thing. The thing that Astrid needed to hear.

"You are Astrid," she said. "Just Astrid. To me you're not the general. You're not the leader of a revolution. I don't know everything the Chancellor has done or why the T.A.L.W. was formed. I don't understand any of it." Sparrow's heart beat so hard it felt like her entire chest was pulsing. She was dying to reach out and touch Astrid. Just touch her, feel her. "I don't even care about it."

"What do you care about?"

Sparrow moved slowly, giving Astrid every chance to pull away. She took hold of one of Astrid's hands and pulled off her glove. Astrid's breath hitched as Sparrow put Astrid's bare hand against her chest. She wanted her to feel her heart beat.

"This is what you are to me." She was beyond caring what was appropriate or not. "This is all I care about."

Astrid's hand shook and she pulled it from Sparrow's grip. There was anguish in her eyes. Still she said nothing. All she did was stare. As if she could finally see her. Then a shadow fell over Astrid's face. She pulled away. *No, come back.*

"I'm so grateful to have Isabeau back, you won't believe it." She went back to the wine bottle and retook her place on the bed. Sparrow could only watch as Astrid put the bottle to her lips again. All she could hear was her own heart. "When she was caught I felt so helpless. She's been with me since the beginning."

"How did the two of you meet?" Sparrow found a coin on the table and started spinning it.

"Like how I meet most of my captains," Astrid said. "When you sign up to kill bad people, once the bullets have been spent, usually the people left standing can be recruited." She laughed mirthlessly.

Sparrow thought about the story that Bianca had told. Maybe she understood what Astrid was telling her. It was like that with her, too. She was still standing when the bombs fell. And here she was now.

"I want you to make me a captain." The words felt wrong and still she said them. "I want to be one of *yours*." Her cheeks heated at the words.

"You're my rat catcher." Astrid snorted. "I don't need you closer to the fight than that."

"But why?"

"Why what?" Astrid grabbed the bottle again. "You should never bet something you're not willing to lose." Sparrow's head spun. What was Astrid saying? "A fight is coming," Astrid continued. "A battle we have no way of preparing for." She locked gazes with Sparrow. "I've doomed us. We only have Anchorage; the Chancellor has the entire country."

"You must have a plan?" Sparrow asked.

Astrid waved the wine bottle enough so that some spilled onto the floor. "I must have, once. I think." Her shoulders sank together and she lay down on the bed.

"You just feel lost right now." Sparrow tried. She looked at the wine puddle on the floor. "Or maybe it's the wine. Or perhaps you—"

"Shut up, rat catcher." Her voice was low and in spite of her words, full of affection, she turned on her side and propped herself up on her elbow. "Come here."

Sparrow got up from the chair, hurrying to get to Astrid's side. She lay down on the small flimsy bed. *The last time we were in bed together was at the House.* It was a strange thought. It was a different world, a different life, and yet they were here together.

"I'm so happy you're here," Astrid whispered. "I'm so happy you're back."

Her words surprised and warmed Sparrow. "I'm happy I'm here, too."

Something glimmered in Astrid's eyes and the look made Sparrow break. There was pain in there, weariness, sadness, and age. Also fire. It reminded Sparrow that she didn't actually know Astrid. She didn't know what Astrid was capable of or what she'd done in the past. Stories that Bianca had told her flew through her mind.

"Astrid?"

Astrid was staring at her lips now. Sparrow could feel her *gaze* on her skin as well as any kiss. She felt like she was igniting. She was panting now, chest heaving, embarrassed by her physical reaction. Astrid was still staring at her, devouring her with just her eyes. "If you need me to stop..." Astrid sounded out of breath. "Tell me, okay. Just tell me if you need—" She reached up and pushed on Sparrow's shoulder until she landed on her back. Astrid leaned over her.

Astrid didn't let Sparrow think or process what was happening before attacking her mouth with a hunger that seemed to surprise both of them. She nipped at Sparrow's lower lips and lapped at her mouth until Sparrow was so out of breath she felt like she was drowning.

It didn't take long for Sparrow to wrap her arms around Astrid's neck. Their kisses were sloppy, hurried, and tasted of wine. Sparrow didn't think she'd ever felt something so perfect. She wanted them to go slow, to go easier on each other. To slow down Astrid so that it no longer felt like a battle. Like they weren't attacking each other.

Astrid would have none of it. She grabbed both of Sparrow's wrists and placed them over Sparrow's head. With her other hand, she pulled Sparrow's shirt out of her trousers and worked her way inside. Sparrow knew what was coming next and she felt dizzy with anticipation. Astrid had never touched her before now and Sparrow wanted it slower so she could savor it.

Her legs were giving out and her head bumped against the wall. The skillful fingers that moved against her were going to make her come faster than she ever had before. She could already feel her lower belly trembling.

Please slow down. She tried to get the words out but they either got stuck or Astrid didn't care. Astrid didn't slow down. When Astrid added a second finger, Sparrow's back arched and instead of screaming, she bit a hold of the creamy skin of Astrid's neck. It was quick and intense, bordering on painful.

"Astrid, Astrid, Astrid." Sparrow could only whimper her name. "Please." *Please don't stop. Please love me. Please, please, please.* The pleading continued in her head as the world turned white and she came around Astrid's fingers.

Sparrow's entire body felt like pudding and she barely registered as Astrid moved down her body and pulled off her trousers.

*

Sparrow must've fallen asleep because suddenly light shone through the cracks in the wooden wall. They were both naked and one of Astrid's legs lay across Sparrow's stomach in a possessive fashion. *Her skin is so beautiful,* Sparrow thoughts as she let her fingers trace the length of Astrid's leg, causing visible goose bumps. There was something comical about the general being ticklish.

Sparrow stopped looking at Astrid's leg and instead focused on her face. She looked younger now. Innocent. And very beautiful. Sparrow reached out and traced her eyebrows and her lips. She both wanted and didn't want Astrid to wake up, and when one blue eye opened, a thrill went through her.

"Good mo—" Sparrow was shut up by a finger on her lips.

Astrid leaned forward and kissed her, pushing and pulling until their bodies were fully aligned again. One of Astrid's legs was still wrapped around her waist.

I love you.

Chapter Twenty-Five

When Sparrow woke up, Astrid wasn't there. She was alone, the sheet rough against her back. Her body ached, but her heart felt light. Like everything was right. It was still raining outside, drops hitting the roof. But it sounded like fine rain and it seemed fitting for the morning.

I should get my clothes, she thought. In that moment, the door opened and Astrid entered.

She was wearing armor and her weapon was attached to her back. She looked proper. Not like she'd been drunk just a few hours before. *Or had it been more than a few hours?* Sparrow felt like she'd slept for several days.

"Where were you?" She sat up, keeping the sheet up past her chest.

Astrid shook her head, leaned down, and pressed a quick kiss to Sparrow's lips. "Duties are boring. Focus on breakfast instead."

That's when Sparrow noticed a small parcel in one of Astrid's hands.

"Breakfast in bed, how special." Sparrow caught the package and opened it. Inside there was a chunk of bread and a piece of ham. At the sight, Sparrow's mouth watered. She was starving.

Without waiting, she ate all of it, naked in bed. There was no reason to stand on ceremony. Not in front of Astrid anyway.

"I thought you might be hungry." Astrid sat down on the stool opposite of the bed. "Especially after—"

"I love you."

The words fell to the floor between them, leaving only silence. Astrid's body went stiff and she leaned backwards. Her gaze went cloudy. Sparrow knew it was a mistake before the words were uttered. She knew she shouldn't have said it. But it was deeper than the truth. It had been the truth for a long time. For months. Since the first time the Madam had sent Astrid to her. With her body bare, eating breakfast in Astrid's bed, what else could she have done?

"Well." Astrid stood up. "I have a meeting to tend to." With that, she got up and left through the door.

Sparrow stared at the closed door. She swallowed, her throat dry. *I should get up.* She should leave. She shouldn't, couldn't, *wouldn't* be there when Astrid came back.

When she grabbed her trousers from the floor and pulled them over her legs, the first tears dropped. She fell to her knees and lifted her hands to cradle her face as hard sobs wrecked through her body.

*

It felt wrong to leave what had felt like a sanctuary at first. She made sure that her face was dry and any signs of crying were gone. She was struggling. She didn't know what the right thing to do was. *Should I pretend like nothing has happened? Should I confront Astrid?* Sparrow even thought of leaving Anchorage for a second but all those thoughts went out the window when she saw Astrid standing not far away, looking at the horses.

It was as if a demon took hold of Sparrow's body. She walked up to Astrid in a few quick strides. "I thought

193

you had a meeting." She sounded pissed off and she didn't care. "Or isn't that what you said."

"What I do, doesn't concern you."

The words stunned Sparrow. "Why are you acting like you hate me?"

Astrid glanced at her then. "I don't care enough to hate you."

Her words slashed Sparrow's heart into shreds. It felt like it would fall. Who was this person? Was this the same person that Sparrow had comforted in the cave? Was it the same person that shared Sparrow's body and heart just a few hours earlier? The same person who brought her breakfast?

"I don't know who you're trying to lie to," Sparrow said. "Me or yourself." She scoffed. "What did you think? That I was going to be your personal concubine? You forgot that I'm human, too."

When Astrid looked at her now, Sparrow was taken aback. Astrid's eyes looked cold, unfeeling. Gray rather than blue.

Astrid breathed calmly and crossed her arms over her chest. "I'm sorry if I disappointed you. I never promised you anything."

*

Sparrow didn't bother to find a tent for the night. It wasn't raining and either way, she wasn't planning on sleeping. Instead she walked past old Anchorage and found the path up to the cliff that she found last time she was here. She sat there, watching the sun set, watching the place of death. She couldn't see New Anchorage from up here, and that was just as well. She didn't want to see anything other than treetops.

I don't care enough to hate you. Astrid's words echoed in her head. Why had she said that? Sparrow knew it wasn't true. She knew that Astrid had to care.

She lay down on the cliff and put one hand on her stomach and the other under her head. It was still cloudy above but now and then the sky broke through, revealing a million twinkling stars. The dew had settled and it was completely dark. A chill settled in the mountain and the forest, and Sparrow started shaking. She knew she couldn't stay up there, but she also couldn't go back down. She was stuck in the middle, her heart refusing to let her go anywhere. She shook as another gust wind hit her. It wasn't summer anymore. *If I stay here all night, I'll freeze to death.*

The thought made her stand up. It was completely dark and the trip down the path was difficult. She held out her hands, worried she was going to fall and break her neck. She needed to leave Anchorage; she knew that now. Astrid didn't want her to be a captain. She also didn't *love* Sparrow the way Sparrow loved her. She had no reason to stay. She didn't want to be a refugee. And she didn't want to hear Astrid call her *rat catcher* one more time.

"I'm not a child," Sparrow told the dark as she stopped at the end of a path. "I'm not an animal keeper. I'm not a captain." She didn't know what she was yet. But she couldn't stay here to find out. When she got out of the forest and into the clearing that was Old Anchorage, it was easier to see. She walked towards the gates.

She didn't know where she was going. Maybe she would try to find Fordon's house. She was sure they'd take her in and if not them, she'd find somewhere else. She'd run away once before and that worked out well. She found *Anchorage*. This time she would—

"Where are you going?"

Where had Astrid come from?

Sparrow spun around and there she was. Standing there. As if she'd been waiting for Sparrow to show up. Sparrow hadn't even heard her come up behind her.

"I'm sure I could spare a horse if you're so adamant on leaving." When Sparrow didn't reply, Astrid sighed. "I don't mean to tell you what to do. It would be a pity for you to wind up dead in a ditch after all this."

"After all this?" Sparrow swallowed back tears.

"You've survived a lot," Astrid looked down. *Was she ashamed?* "That's all I mean."

Sparrow shivered when another cold wind swirled around them. She didn't know what to say. Her emotions felt numb.

"I'm sorry, okay?" Astrid cleared her throat. "Just don't do this. Don't leave like this in the middle of the night. If you want to leave, I'll have someone escort you somewhere tomorrow. I don't want you to die."

"You said you didn't care about me." Sparrow crossed her arms over her chest. "So why does it matter to you if I die?"

"Of course I care." Astrid sounded like a child being told off. "I just... You were right, I used you. I didn't treat you like a person with feelings. I'm sorry."

Something about this didn't feel like an apology and Sparrow felt anger rise. "I don't accept your apology."

"That's fine," Astrid said. "You don't need to. I just needed to say it. And it won't happen again." She sighed before continuing. "I didn't realize what I was doing. I was making you mine and that's not fair. I'm a dead woman walking, Sparrow." The use of her own name stumped Sparrow. "I didn't mean for you to fall in love with me. I didn't mean to care about you. I only have one function in this life and that's to bring down the Chancellor and hopefully kill him with my own two hands. My function is to liberate. Not to love. Not to *be* with you."

"I've loved you since before AngelGarden." Sparrow's voice broke. "You didn't even need to try."

Astrid chuckled, but it was a sad sound. Not a happy one. "I didn't mean to," Astrid said. "You made me forget everything for a moment. You made me stop hurting and if I forget and stop feeling this rage and this pain, I can't do my job."

"Maybe it's okay to be human from time to time, you know?" Sparrow's anger was dissipating. Now she was just sad. The pain that Astrid carried wasn't normal. Not natural. Not good.

"Perhaps." Astrid's facial expression was hidden in the darkness. "But I don't just belong to myself. My job is too important." She shook her head as if getting rid of thoughts and emotions. "I need your help."

"*My* help?"

"Yes." Astrid said. "And it can't wait. I've already called the majority of my captains; I just needed to get you."

Sparrow pouted, grateful that Astrid couldn't see her face. "Is that why you asked me to stay?"

"No," Astrid said. "If you want to leave tomorrow, I will *help* you, not *stop* you. And you don't have to come to the meeting if you don't want to. You have your own free will. But you asked me yesterday to make you a captain. I don't want you to be a captain, but I found a way you can help. A way you can *really* help. If I know you, and I think I do, you won't say no."

Sparrow sighed. Of course Astrid was right.

Chapter Twenty-Six

Sparrow hadn't known there were that many captains. They were inside a bigger building, organized like a church with six rows of benches. Every row held at least 10 captains. Sparrow's eyes went wide as Astrid pulled her to the front row and sat her down next to *Isabeau.*

"Hi," Sparrow whispered. "I'm glad to see you're here."

"Thanks." Isabeau didn't smile but it was close enough.

"There's so many people here." Astrid still hadn't started talking. "I didn't know there were that many captains."

Isabeau snorted. "Not everyone's here. There are 70 captains all in all." She grimaced. "70 people do not make an army."

Sparrow felt her cheeks heat in embarrassment. At the House she'd never seen that many people in the same room before. She opened her mouth to answer but then Astrid began speaking.

"I'm not going to waste any time on pleasantries," Astrid said. She was standing on a podium. Next to her was a table with some sort of white structure on it. From where she was seated, Sparrow couldn't tell what it was. "We are here to plan a strike on the Chancellor, one that he will never forget." Somebody whistled in the back. "He came here and he bombed *us.*" Astrid was shining. Sparrow had never seen her like this before. "He tried to kill *us.* We need to strike now. Show him that we are a force to be reckoned with. That the *T.A.L.W.* is still here and here to stay. That if he's going to attack us, he better kill all of us because like *cockroaches..."* Astrid's eyes glittered. "...all it takes is one and soon you'll have another colony to deal with." Some people laughed which told Sparrow that it wasn't the first time the cockroach analogy had been used.

"What are we going to do?" A man yelled from somewhere near Sparrow.

Astrid took a deep breath. "We are going to *bomb* AngelGarden."

Sparrow's breath hitched and she almost started coughing. AngelGarden. The garden of skeletons. The roof. The maze. Rufus. A murmur made its way through the crowd.

"AngelGarden has housed the first family since the Chancellor himself ordered the attack on the capital," Astrid said. "They kept one of our captains prisoner for days. Tortured and starved her." Astrid was looking at Isabeau now. "We need to bring AngelGarden down. Preferably tomorrow but the day after is fine, too." She took a deep breath. "I'm going to ask you all to leave in a few moments so that I can discuss the details with Captain Tillgadd, Captain Fordon, and our newest captain." Sparrow's heart skipped a beat. Had Astrid changed her mind?" "Captain Stephen." A thin red haired man, who'd been leaning against the opposite wall, took a step forward and nodded. Sparrow was surprised she hadn't seen him standing there before. "I'll call the rest of you at daybreak. Then we'll be ready." She excused them and one by one, they all left.

Isabeau stayed seated and Sparrow stayed as well. She didn't think that Astrid had called her to that meeting just to tell her they were bombing AngelGarden. As soon as

200

the last captains left, Astrid nodded for Isabeau and Sparrow. Fordon came from the back of the room. As soon as she saw Sparrow she smiled, reached out, and squeezed her shoulder. It was sweet.

"How is Bianca?"

Fordon's smile disappeared. "Not very well. I'm not sure why but she's not sleeping properly."

Sparrow gritted her teeth. She didn't like the thought of being unable to comfort Bianca. She wanted the girl to be okay.

"As soon as I can..." Sparrow answered. "I'm going to visit her."

"I think she'd like that." Fordon and Sparrow stopped by the table where Astrid stood.

Sparrow could now see what the white structure was. It was a model of AngelGarden—white walls, garden and all.

"Okay." Astrid got their attention back. "I want to carry out this attack as soon as possible." She put both palms on the table. "We got Isabeau out of there, and we managed to get back here. We need to do this before the Chancellor attacks again." Fordon, Isabeau, Stephen, and Sparrow stood around the table, all of them looking at her. "Stephen, I don't know if you've met the others but this is your time to shine." Her gaze met Sparrow's. "Captain Stephen has access to a plane and explosives. He will fly the plane over AngelGarden. His plane doesn't have an automatic bomb system so Fordon, you and Isabeau will drop the bombs physically."

His plane. Sparrow remembered the talk with the doctor all those weeks ago. Was this the secret mission that Astrid had been on? To procure a plane for the T.A.L.W.?

No wonder Astrid had been so excited about it. The Chancellor would never see that coming.

"What about me?" Sparrow asked. "What do you need me to do?"

"I want to slit the Chancellor's throat before the bombing," Astrid said. She looked right at her. "I want you to guide me to his bedroom. I can't risk getting lost in the maze."

They all spoke at once.

"What?"

"Are you crazy?"

"You can't be serious!"

"Astrid, for goodness sake," Isabeau said. "Bombing AngelGarden will be enough! Don't put yourself and Sparrow in danger."

"If I don't do it," Astrid said, "he will survive somehow. He's like a snake. I won't believe it unless I see the light go out in his eyes myself."

"So why bomb the place at all?" The pieces didn't fit together in Sparrow's head. She didn't mean to question the leader of the T.A.L.W. but here she was.

"To kill the family and send a message. Waerdarei lives. And will be liberated." Astrid crossed her hands over her chest. "It's decided. Sparrow and I infiltrate the building and slit the throat of that vile man. As soon as we get out, we light a beacon. Stephen, Fordon, and Isabeau: you will be flying nearby and as soon as you see the beacon, you bomb the place. The rest of the army we've divided into two. Half will stay here so that we don't leave New Anchorage completely defenseless. The others will wait in the ditches, ready to kill anything or anyone that escapes the house alive. I want everyone dead." Her eyes sparkled and thrills went down Sparrow's spine. She didn't allow herself to look away. This was Astrid. Sparrow was adamant on loving all of her whether Astrid wanted her to or not. Whether Astrid scared her or not.

"How will you get into AngelGarden?" Isabeau looked at the small replica in front of them. "We all know the way to the main door but we need to get through it somehow. I'm sure there's more security now than when we left, not less."

Sparrow bit her lip, gathering courage. Maybe this was her time to shine. "I might have an idea."

All eyes landed on her.

Chapter Twenty-Seven

This is never going to work. The closer they got to AngelGarden, the faster Sparrow's heart beat. Every rock, every tree, every patch of gravel felt familiar. Even though she was wearing armor this time and walking instead of riding, Sparrow was constantly reminded of last time. She tried to keep her gaze on Astrid's back to make herself stay focused. They both wore all black, trying to blend in with the dark trees.

Occasionally, Sparrow thought she could hear engines and wondered if it was Stephen's plane carrying Fordon, Isabeau, and lots of explosives. Explosives that would soon rain over AngelGarden.

They were close now. The white building towered in front of them. Sparrow had gone numb even though she was vaguely aware of her heart fluttering in her chest like a trapped bird.

You know you're able to say no, Astrid had told her before leaving. *I won't look down on you if you say no.* But of course Sparrow had said yes. Come hell or high water, she would die helping Astrid rather than not help her.

"Come on." Astrid gestured for her to follow.

They crouched and moved towards the front door on their hands and feet. They were kept hidden thanks to the dark and the bumps and rocks on the ground. Sparrow's heart was beating harder and harder, making her entire body shake. Two guards stood by the door; they hadn't been there when Sparrow, Bianca, and Isabeau had run in the middle of the night. They wore the black colors of the Amelioratites.

There's a man sized vent near the kitchen door. That's what Rufus had said. Now Sparrow just had to find it. They crawled to the side of the house, slowly, avoiding any twig or rubble that might produce extra noise. A part of Sparrow was surprised they'd gotten this far at all.

They found the kitchen door. While Sparrow continued forward to find the vent, Astrid stood up and tried the door handle.

What? She mouthed when Sparrow gave her a look. "I had to try," she whispered.

Sparrow shook her head and chuckled. She turned back to the wall, and there, next to it, close to the ground, was a vent. She took a small knife from her belt and pried it off the tunnel. Astrid came and stood next to her.

"Ah," Astrid whispered. "There we go." She looked at Sparrow. "You're up, rat catcher. Catch me the biggest rat there is."

Sparrow nodded. The fear was dissipating and being replaced with another feeling. A feeling Sparrow wasn't used to. It was a mix of anticipation and blood lust. She *wanted* to see Astrid kill him. Even if it was the last thing they ever did.

In front of them was a pitch black tunnel. There was nothing to do but move forward. Sparrow went ahead, taking comfort in the fact that Astrid was right behind her. They followed the tunnel going upwards, steps etched onto the side. It was easy to climb. The tunnel widened until they were in front of a door. A normal door without a lock. "Is this where the maze starts?"

Sparrow nodded. She put her hand around the handle and opened the door.

They were in a room Sparrow had never been in before. She'd never been that deep in the maze. It was an oval room, with no less than 16 doors. There was no time to waste. She walked over to the first door and inspected the handle. It had a small chip of bronze paint on it, but Sparrow wasn't going to choose a door until she looked at all the handles.

"This one." She stopped by the fifth door. She could always be wrong of course; there was a possibility that Rufus hadn't told her everything. Her gut feeling told her otherwise.

She opened the door and they walked through it. This room, she did recognize. The smell more than anything. If she was correct, after this room, there would only be corridors. The light was dim, but Sparrow recognized the pile in the middle of the room. The room smelled of death and Sparrow knew that the pile in the middle was remains. Remains of *something* or *someone.*

"Let's get out of here," Sparrow said and grabbed Astrid's hand. This time she found the correct door easily. It was on the opposite side.

The air grew thicker inside the maze Sparrow's heart continued fluttering like a captive bird. She hated this feeling. *I'm here with Astrid,* she tried to tell herself but it didn't help. With every door, Sparrow got less and less sure of the method. All the corridors looked the same to her.

She had almost given up when the final door opened and they were out of the maze.

"Good job," Astrid whispered behind her.

"What do we do about the wife?" Sparrow hadn't thought about it before, but surely the wife would be there, too.

"We need to silence her as fast as possible," Astrid said. "I've killed spouses before. Usually the wife runs out screaming or sits apathetic in the corner; I'm sure she won't be a problem." Her tone was matter-of-fact and the fabric of Astrid's jacket was cool under Sparrow's fingers. *She's probably ice to the core.* You had to be in order to kill.

"I can try to help." Sparrow touched her fingers to the knife hanging in her belt.

Astrid nodded. "Let's go then."

Sparrow went first as they skulked down the corridor. Sparrow was grateful for the dark. She didn't want to look at the strange painted flowers. When they passed by the portrait of an angel weeping, she knew they were going the right way. When they passed by Rufus's bedroom, she slowed down further, listening, waiting. It felt like any minute, Rufus could barge out of the room and find them.

Sparrow glanced back, looking at Astrid. She couldn't believe this was where her life had led her. She crept forward until they reached a double door with gold handles. *Could this be it?* It wasn't the dining room; it wasn't a bathroom; it wasn't Rufus's room or the study. This had to be it. They stopped and Sparrow nodded. Her heart slowed. She felt peaceful. Ready. *Come what may.* She didn't know what waited for them on the other side, but she was ready for all of it.

Astrid took her hand and linked their fingers together. She took Sparrow's hand to her lips and pressed a kiss to it. Then she let go of Sparrow's hand and nodded.

Here we go.

It felt like time stood still. Sparrow opened the door and Astrid sauntered inside, her movements fluid. Sparrow closed the door behind them but couldn't take her eyes off Astrid. It looked like she was dancing. She walked over to the wife first, looking at her neck and then scanning the rest of her body. Ruby, his wife, was fast asleep, one leg and one arm outside the cover. The soft skin of her inner arm shone in the dark, white like the skeleton garden outside. Without a warning Astrid took out her knife and with a swift movement cut a line from her shoulder to her hand. The wife made a moan and blood splashed on the floor. Astrid must've cut off an important artery. Sparrow took a few steps forward. She was morbidly curious and wanted to see better.

"Ruby?" The Chancellor spoke. "Ruby are you okay?"

Astrid grinned and jumped on top of the bed, straddling the Chancellor and pushing him into the mattress. She dropped the knife on the floor and took out her rifle, placing it against his temple. Sparrow hurried to pick up the knife. It was red with blood and she wiped it on the sheet.

"So here we are," Astrid's tone was low.

"Here we are," the Chancellor said. He glanced toward the side. "What did you do to my wife?"

"She's dead," Astrid said. "But don't worry, I made it quick. She bled out within seconds."

"Ruby." The Chancellor sighed and shook his head. "I'm sorry, Ruby." He didn't sound like someone who'd just lost his life partner.

"Stop talking to her." Astrid unfastened the security on her weapon. "Talk to me. I'm here now. The dog leader of the revolution. I bested you. I did this. *I* did this."

"It appears that you did," the Chancellor said. "Killing me won't fix all your problems, I hope you know that. I'm just one person. My party still exists. My ideals will live on without me."

Ruby's blood trickled toward Sparrow and she made a small squeak and jumped backwards. This made both Astrid and the Chancellor look up. The Chancellor's eyes went wide.

"You!" He said. "You little piece of—"

Bam! Astrid pulled the trigger and blew his brains out. The sound echoed in the small room.

"You don't talk to her." Astrid hit his chest with the butt of the rifle.

"Astrid, come on." Sparrow ran up to her and grabbed her hand. The sound had been so loud it must've been heard by others. She pulled Astrid off the bed and they leapt for the door. They needed to get out of this house of terror and death.

They made it to the kitchen without being stopped and Astrid kicked open the door. Within minutes they were out in the open, running through the field of orange flowers that made it look like the ground was on fire.

Sparrow's blood fizzed and laughter bubbled through her chest. She couldn't believe they managed to get in and out without being killed. They ran hand in hand through the courtyard. Something was happening in Sparrow's body. She remembered this feeling. A feeling that she'd forgotten. She was once a child. She'd played like this. Running. Being pursued. She had friends and they played. Before the House.

They ran up the hill near AngelGarden. Astrid let go of Sparrow's hand and threw herself on the ground. She lit the beacon and it shone in the sky.

"Come on." She was out of breath. "Let's get higher so we can watch."

They didn't need to run anymore. Instead, they climbed at their own pace as they heard the plane getting closer. Sparrow felt like she was lit on fire and when they finally sat down on the top of the hill, she was shaking uncontrollably.

"Here, try to calm down." Astrid pulled her close and put her arms around Sparrow's shoulders. "You're okay. You did well."

The plane was right over AngelGarden now and the first bomb fell. Sparrow watched it fall and dug her fingers into the fabric of Astrid's trousers. The ground shook as it hit and somebody screamed. Astrid held her tighter. Another bomb fell and a whole wing tumbled to the ground. Dust and soot turned the sky even darker and fire scented the air. *The garden can't be white anymore.* Another bomb fell. And then another and another. The entire AngelGarden was up in flames. People were screaming. Sparrow wasn't sad about the carnage. It felt righteous. Justified.

"Astrid, do you—" Sparrow couldn't finish her sentence before Astrid was kissing her. Kissing her deeply, completely. Tugging on her shirt. Sparrow was all too eager to comply. If Astrid wanted to take her right here, Sparrow would let her. When the sun set the next day AngelGarden would be gone, the world would be different, and Sparrow was Astrid's.

Epilogue

"Stop. You're tickling me." But Astrid didn't stop. She kept her touch feather light and ran her fingers over the back of Sparrow's arms. *It's as if she* wants *to torture me,* Sparrow thought with a chuckle. She turned around and pushed Astrid's hands away. She stretched her body and pressed a quick kiss to Astrid's lips. "Good morning."

Astrid smiled. For once, Astrid's skin was warm and rosy, her eyes closer to warm indigo than ice. Sparrow wanted to keep her in here, in their shack in New Anchorage. She pulled her down for more kisses, their naked bodies aligning. It was hard to imagine that it was snowing outside when it was so warm under the cover.

"We'll have to go outside eventually, you know," Astrid said when they came up for air. "The rest of the T.A.L.W. will wonder what you've done to their general."

Sparrow propped herself up on her elbow and leaned over Astrid. She started tracing circles around Astrid's belly-button. "And what have I done to their general then?" She reached lower, enjoying the way Astrid's eyelids grew heavy. "Tell me in detail."

Astrid grinned. "I think it's either some spell or poison." She closed her eyes. Sparrow had to kiss her again. "Mmm, you are so delicious."

Sparrow laughed. "Says you."

She sat up, stretched her back, and looked around the room. Sunlight peeked through the crack on the other side of the wall. On the table next to the bed, there was an empty bowl. Last night it had been filled with cherries, a

211

gift from Astrid. Sparrow smiled at the memory of eating them. Astrid still remembering that cherries were her favorite was so sweet.

Sparrow sighed. She knew that it wouldn't always be like this. That any minute now, Astrid would decide that they'd been in there long enough and they'd have to leave. But unlike before, Sparrow wasn't worried. Even if Astrid hadn't told her she loved her yet, Sparrow knew that she did. Or something close to it. Sparrow felt it in Astrid's gaze, in her kisses, and the way she hadn't let Sparrow out of her sight since the fall of AngelGarden.

"We have to go out soon, don't we?" Astrid's smile was unreadable but very comforting. She reached out and touched Sparrow's hair, tugged on it.

"We do," Astrid answered. Her smile disappeared and she sat up. "I've really enjoyed these days though."

Her words warmed Sparrow's chest. "Me too."

"The fight isn't over," Astrid continued. "And I still have to lead the T.A.L.W."

"You're still the general." Sparrow nodded then she grinned. "And I'm still a rat catcher."

Astrid laughed.

About the Author

Kathy grew up travelling around the world but is now settled with her wife in Sweden. By day she is a primary school teacher, by night, a writer, and with the little spare time she has left she enjoys cooking, playing video games and spending time with her family.

Other Titles Available From
Triplicity Publishing

Crossed Reins by Graysen Morgen. Barrel racing is Carly Rae Walsh's life, until it's ripped out from under her. With nothing to do and nothing to lose, she uses her years of horse whispering skills and intuition to train a troubled thoroughbred race horse. Allison McKinley is a world class dressage rider who has stepped back from the spotlight to mourn the sudden death of her mother. The last thing she needs when she decides to start training again for competition, is her father's impulsive desire to own a race horse, and his bizarre decision to choose a rodeo barrel racer as the trainer. The two women have nothing in common except horses, and even that's a stretch. Can they uncross the reins long enough to see what's happening between them?

Outside In by Breanna Hughes. Cali Evans is a survivor. Her life hasn't been easy, but her late father raised her to be smart, tough, and dependent only on herself and her wits. On the eve of her 21st birthday she meets Owen Bray - a beautiful and intriguing young doctor who equally frustrates and captivates Cali. That fateful meeting inspires Cali to make a better life for herself. The next day, hoping to make positive change, Cali hops a bus for the West Coast but never reaches her destination. Instead, she wakes up in an underground bunker with no recollection of how she got there. Upon her arrival, she learns that she's one of just forty survivors of a fast-spreading environmental toxin and that human life outside of the bunker has ceased to exist. Tired of the vague explanations and half-answers coming from the people in charge, Cali takes it upon herself to investigate the real reason why she's there and begins to uncover the sinister truth.

I Love You, Nora Whispered by Kathy L. Salt. Love in the time of horses and polio. England, 1948. Nora Lakes suffers from post polio syndrome and very low self-esteem. When her sister Martha manages to get her a job at Waterhouse Acre Stables, she can hardly believe it. She had never imagined that anyone would have employed her, damaged as she is. She also never imagined she would meet anybody like Katherine. Katherine Waterhouse was born with a silver spoon in her mouth. She has a mean streak and doesn't like people in general. What she does like, is horses. She wants to be a professional rider but growing up in a conservative house where her choices are limited by her sex, Katherine has always been trapped in her role as a woman. Nora and Katherine - two women with very different backgrounds, drawn to each other with an intensity neither of them are prepared for. Do they stand a chance?

Omega Rising by Domina Alexandra. A few months of peace. That was all Bonnie Collins was granted. New trouble has surfaced and go figure, this trouble came with a new pair of claws. When an unknown pack comes to town, Bonnie is forced to make tough decisions that will influence her packs future. Things only get harder when her mate is taken, leaving Bonnie in charge of a pack who still doesn't trust her. With chaos all around, it will be exactly what Bonnie needs to finally embrace what she has become. An Omega Rising. Book 2 of the *Claimed Series*.

Loose Ends by Joan L. Anderson. After her estranged sister is killed when she falls onto the subway tracks in Paris just as a train arrives, Allison goes to Paris to deal with her sister's body and collect her things. But, after talking to the police about the accident and viewing the subway surveillance video, something seems odd about her death. When Allison's hotel room in Paris is broken into with only a few things taken, but not any money or credit cards, she begins to wonder if it really was an accident that killed her sister, or if it was murder. Once Allison returns to Washington, D.C. to handle her sister's affairs, she soon realizes that her sister had been living a secret life and wasn't the person she had always thought she was. As troubling things begin to happen to Allison in D.C., she starts wondering if she will be the next person to die.

Real Love by Graysen Morgen. Leigh Myer is a trauma nurse practitioner who is not happy going through the motions of her daily life. When a friend offers up her mountain cabin for a relaxing vacation, Leigh packs her bags. She's never been to the mountains and certainly never in heavy snow. A chance meeting with a fish and wildlife officer turns her idea of a quiet, relaxing vacation…upside down. Camden Gorely loves her job and loves the mountain she works and lives on even more. She's tired of having flings with vacationers who visit for days or weeks at a time, until she meets the elusive nurse from the city. Can Leigh stop running from her past and allow real love into her heart?

Enticed by Love by Lynn Lawler. Henrietta Bailey is a mysterious woman who has spent her entire life living in the town of Crescent, a sleepy beach community in central coastal California. She loves the beach, the ocean air, and the town itself. Her simple life fulfills her. However, she spends much of her time reminiscing about her long-lost love, a woman who left her devastated. Now, another woman awaits on the horizon; a wise, intelligent, and sexy lady who is sophisticated beyond her years. This woman yearns for her soul mate and lover. Will she be able to win Henrietta's heart, or will Henrietta be fated to live the rest of her days alone?

Love Undercover by Domina Alexandra. Remi Stone never expected to get the opportunity to work undercover for narcotics. But, when the chance arrives, she takes it. With drugs coursing through a high school, Remi has only until the end of the school year to find the suspects responsible. Undercover, Remi plays her role, moving one step further into the drug industry. She never thought she'd be moving one step closer to the woman who would change her life and take hold of her heart. There is just one issue. Remi Stone is undercover as an eighteen year old high school senior. And the woman she can't seem to ignore is her History teacher. There will be a lot of challenges along the way, including one that could cost Remi her life and her heart.

Playing the Game by Graysen Morgen. Randi Rojas is a professional soccer player who seemingly has it all, a successful career, a long-term girlfriend, a loving family, and a great group of friends…until a chance meeting with an attractive woman sends her way offside, and into a whole new game. Berkley Ward lives her life to the extreme, spending her days either in the gym or four-wheeling in the woods, and her nights patrolling the streets as an officer. Affairs with taken women are easy, but after years of playing games, she's finished…until she meets a beautiful woman and a game she can't resist. Both women play a dangerously seductive game of cat and mouse, teetering on the edge of friendship and affair.

Rebel Sweetheart by Sydney Canyon. When a headstrong, country music superstar starts getting threatening letters while on tour, her manager has no other choice but to hire someone to investigate the threats, and keep her safe. Haley Nielsen is as stubborn as it gets. She does things her way, and her way only. The last thing she needs or wants is a babysitter following her every move and controlling everything she does. Shane Crowley isn't your typical private investigator, or bodyguard, for that matter. She's a former U.S. Deputy Marshal with a lot of experience, and an all or nothing attitude. Tempers flare and the energy burns red hot between the two women as they spend weeks together cooped up on Haley's tour bus, traveling the country. Will they stop resisting each other long enough to see eye to eye? Or will the letter writer make good on his threats?

A Tale of Spiders and Canned Soup by Kathy L. Salt. Living on your own can be hard, but even more so when you're dealing with haphephobia; the death of a twin sister; and a crush on your teacher. Mika is still in contact with her foster family who homes the loves of her life, three young children she would do anything for, when she begins attending University of Aberdeen and meets Pauline, an Australian that teaches Viking history. Neither woman is used to breaking the rules, and their way to each other is a hard one, especially when Mika vows to get custody of the children, whether she is ready to be a parent or not. *A story about growing up. A story about dealing with grief. A story about Mika and Pauline.*

A Night Claimed by Domina Alexandra. Bonnie Collins had plans. And being a werewolf wasn't one of them. Attacked by a rogue who was out to claim her, and facing what she now has no choice of becoming, Bonnie can't let go of her human life as a Paramedic. The last thing Bonnie needs is more challenges. However, Rikki, the Alpha of Mill City will be just that. Finding her to be possessive and ruling, Bonnie begins challenging the Alpha's every breath. Finding out her attack was no accident only makes her more angry at the situation. A group of rogues are out to get her. With no clue why, Bonnie has no choice but to seek help from the alluring Alpha and her pack, accepting the new world she was forced into.

Stunted by Breanna Hughes. Professional stuntwoman Jessie Knight takes her job very seriously and although she works in the entertainment industry, she has zero desire for fame or notoriety. She also has a very strict no-dating policy when it comes to coworkers. That is, until, she meets famous actress Elliot Chase on the set of her new film. The adrenaline rush of the stunts is nothing compared to the sparks that fly between them. After a passionate night together, a sex tape is leaked that sends Jessie and Elliot's private and professional lives into a spiral. Will the fallout be too much for them to last? Or will they find a way out of the mess together?

Mission Compromised by Graysen Morgen. Natalia Moreno is thrilled when she arrives in Fiji for a relaxing vacation. However, she soon discovers the overwater bungalow she's staying in has been double booked for the entire stay, and the resort is full. Annoyed and frustrated, she has no other choice but to share her hut with a stranger. Christian Garnier is sent to Fiji for what she refers to as a working vacation, until she finds out she has an ornery roommate for the next two weeks who is dead set on making her job twice as hard. Soon, all hell breaks loose and the two women are sent around the world on a wild goose chase.

Stargazing by Kathy L. Salt. Lissa stared open-mouthed at the GIF that played over and over on the screen in front of her. Heat flushed to her face, igniting her skin. Her heart started pounding in her chest. *Stupid internet, it should really come with a warning label.* She's never been interested in relationships or sex and as the years have gone by she has retreated more and more into her work. Everything changes when she meets Star, a porn actress with a heart of gold and a troubled childhood. *They say that opposites attract, but how much of that is true? What chance do they have when one of them is a virgin and the other one star in pornography?*

I Belong with Her by Domina Alexandra. Tajel Pierce loves the thrill of being a paramedic. Every call she goes on gives her a rush. She makes no time for a personal life. No one can ruin her love for her career. Then there is Arianna Castaldi, who just transferred to her new paramedic position in a whole new state. All she needs is a new start without any distractions. Arianna and Tajel's relationship doesn't start off perfect. Embarrassed of the one night stand Arianna believes she had with Tajel, she wants to pretend they never met and make their relationship strictly business. The only choice they have to keep from strangling each other is to go from denying their feelings to accepting them as they work through intense 911 calls.

Awakened by Fate by Lynn Lawler. Jackie is a woman living life according to her own rules. She's married, but it's the unspoken, open kind. She can have as many female lovers as she likes; she just can't talk about them. After a bizarre encounter turns her world upside down, things slowly begin to change. She finds herself in desperation as she searches for answers. What she discovers is nothing is delivered in a neatly wrapped box. Now that everything has been brought out into the open, she finds she can't run away from her truth anymore. With her new life, comes new responsibilities and a different outcome than what she was expecting. Jackie isn't alone in the story. She meets several new people who help her along her journey.

Nautical Delights by S. L. Gape. Lady Elizabeth Barrington has spent her entire life trying to please her family; constantly opting for a quiet life, she utilises her profession as a doctor to keep out of her families' clutches; bar the annual two-week Caribbean private cruise, where there is simply no budge. Confined to two weeks on board the Iconica super yacht, she intends on keeping her head down and enjoying as much of the holiday as she can, whilst keeping her family at arm's length. Until a crew member catches her eye.

Worlds Apart by S.L. Gape. Hollywood A-lister Heidi Spencer-Brady is everything you'd expect of an Idol. Loved by all, the British Beauty is graceful, talented, humble and so far removed from the 'typical' LA scene. When her husband's infidelity with his new 'leading lady' is leaked, Dawn, Heidi's best friend and manager, goes all out to protect her. She arranges for Heidi to go back to the UK and stay on her cousins farm they had visited as children, much to the disappointment of the animal fearing Heidi.

Castor Valley (Law & Order Series Book 2) by Graysen Morgen. Jessie Henry is torn when she reads about the capture of the Doyle brothers, two young men who were part of her old gang. Unable to let them hang for a crime she's sure they didn't commit, Jessie leaves her wife and the Town of Boone Creek behind, and sets out on a journey back to the one place she thought she'd never see again, *Castor Valley*. Ellie Henry watches the love of her life leave, not knowing if she will ever return. When she gets an odd telegram, nearly a week later, she fears Jessie is in trouble. With no other choice, she goes to the one person who can help her.

Fight to the Top by S. L. Gape. Georgia is a forty year old, single, Area Director from Manchester, UK who is all work and definitely no play. Having no time to socialise or spend time with her family she prides herself on being fit and well-polished. Erika is an Area Director for the same company, but in the United States. Whilst she is concentrating so heavily on the promotion she has been fighting for, she's starting to feel like her life outside of work is falling apart. The two women are exceptionally different, and worlds apart. Both of their lives are turned upside down when their jobs are snatched from under their noses, and they are suddenly faced with being thrown together by their bosses for one last major project...in Texas.

Boone Creek (Law & Order Series book 1) by Graysen Morgen. Jessie Henry is looking for a new life. She's unknown in the town of Boone Creek when she arrives, and wants to keep it that way. When she's offered the job of Town Marshal, she takes it, believing that protecting others and upholding the law is the penance for her past. Ellie Fray is a widowed, shopkeeper. She generally keeps to herself, but the mysterious new Town Marshal both intrigues and infuriates her. She believes the last thing the town needs is someone stirring up trouble with the outlaws who have taken over.

Witness by Joan L. Anderson. Becca and Kate have lived together for eight years, and have always spent their vacation in a tropical paradise, lying on a beach. This year, Becca wanted to try something different: a seven day, 65-mile hike in the beautiful Cascade Mountains of Washington state. Their peaceful vacation turns to horror when they stumble upon a brutal murder taking place in the back country.

Too Soon by S.L. Gape. Brooke is a twenty-nine year old detective from Oxford, who has her life pretty much planned out until her boss and partner of nine years, Maria, tells her their relationship is over. When Brooke finds out the truth, that Maria cheated on her with their best friend Paula, she decides to get her life back on track by getting away for six weeks in Anglesey, North Wales. Chloe, a thirty three year old artist and art director, owns a log cabin on Anglesey where she spends each weekend painting and surfing. After returning from a surf, she stumbles upon the somewhat uptight and enigmatic Brooke.

Never Quit (Never Series book 2) by Graysen Morgen. Two years after stepping away from the action as a Coast Guard Rescue Swimmer to become an instructor, Finley finds herself in charge of the most difficult class of cadets she's ever faced, while also juggling the taxing demands of having a home life with her partner Nicole, and their fifteen year old daughter. Jordy Ross gave up everything, dropping out of college, and leaving her family behind, to join the Coast Guard and become a rescue swimmer cadet. The extreme training tests her fitness level, pushing her mentally and physically further than she's ever been in her life, but it's the aggressive competition between her and another female cadet that proves to be the most challenging.

Never Let Go (Never Series book 1) by Graysen Morgen. For Coast Guard Rescue Swimmer, Finley Morris, life is good. She loves her job, is well respected by her peers, and has been given an opportunity to take her career to the next level. The only thing missing is the love of her life, who walked out, taking their daughter with her, seven years earlier. When Finley gets a call from her ex, saying their teenage daughter is coming to spend the summer with her, she's floored. While spending more time with her daughter, whom she doesn't get to see often, and learning to be a full-time parent, Finley quickly realizes she has not, and will never, let go of what is important.

Pursuit by Joan L. Anderson. Claire is a workaholic attorney who flies to Paris to lick her wounds after being dumped by her girlfriend of seventeen years. On the plane she chats with the young woman sitting next to her, and when they land the woman is inexplicably detained in Customs. Claire is surprised when she later runs into the woman in the city. They agree to meet for breakfast the next morning, but when the woman doesn't show up Claire goes to her hotel and makes a horrifying discovery. She soon finds herself ensnared in a web of intrigue and international terrorism, becoming the target of a high stakes game of cat and mouse through the streets of Paris.

Wrecked by Sydney Canyon. To most people, the *Duchess* is a myth formed by old pirates tales, but to Reid Cavanaugh, a Caribbean island bum and one of the best divers and treasure hunters in the world, it's a real, seventeenth century pirate ship—the holy grail of underwater treasure hunting. Reid uses the same cunning tactics she always has before setting out to find the lost ship. However, she is forced to bring her business partner's daughter along as collateral this time because he doesn't trust her. Neither woman is thrilled, but being cooped up on a small dive boat for days, forces them to get know each other quickly.

Arson by Austen Thorne. Madison Drake is a detective for the Stetson Beach Police Department. The last thing she wants to do is show a new detective the ropes, especially when a fire investigation becomes arson to cover up a murder. Madison butts heads with Tara, her trainee, deals with sarcasm from Nic, her ex-girlfriend who is a patrol officer, and finds calm in the chaos of police work with Jamie, her best friend who is the county medical examiner. Arson is the first of many in a series of novella episodes surrounding the fictional Stetson Beach Police Department and Detective Madison Drake.

***Mommies (Bridal Series book 3)* by Graysen Morgen.** Britton and her wife Daphne have been married for a year and a half and are happy with their life, until Britton's mother hounds her to find out why her sister Bridget hasn't decided to have children yet. This prompts Daphne to bring up the big subject of having kids of their own with Britton. Britton hadn't really thought much about having kids, but her love for Daphne makes her see life and their future together in a whole new way when they decide to become mommies.

***Rapture & Rogue* by Sydney Canyon.** Taren Rauley is happy and in a good relationship, until the one person she thought she'd never see again comes back into her life. She struggles to keep the past from colliding with the present as old feelings she thought were dead and gone, begin to haunt her. In college, Gianna Revisi was a mastermind, ring-leading, crime boss. Now, she has a great life and spends her time running Rapture and Rogue, the two establishments she built from the ground up. The last person she ever expects to see walk into one of them, is the girl who walked out on her, breaking her heart five years ago.

***Second Chance* by Sydney Canyon.** After an attack on her convoy, Marine Corps Staff Sergeant, Darien Hollister, must learn to live without her sight. When an experimental procedure allows her to see again, Darien is torn, knowing someone had to die in order for this to happen. She embarks on a journey to personally thank the donor's family, but is too stunned to tell them the truth. Mixed emotions stir inside of her as she slowly gets to the know the people that feel like so much more than strangers to her. When the truth finally comes out, Darien walks away, taking the second chance that she's been given to go back to the only life she's ever known, but she's not the only one with a second chance at life.

Meant to Be by Graysen Morgen. Brandt is about to walk down the aisle with her girlfriend, when an unexpected chain of events turns her world upside down, causing her to question the last three years of her life. A chance encounter sparks a mix of rage and excitement that she has never felt before. Summer is living life and following her dreams, all the while, harboring a huge secret that could ruin her career. She believes that some things are better kept in the dark, until she has her third run-in with a woman she had hoped to never see again, and gives into temptation. Brandt and Summer start believing everything happens for a reason as they learn the true meaning of meant to be.

Coming Home by Graysen Morgen. After tragedy derails TJ Abernathy's life, she packs up her three year old son and heads back to Pennsylvania to live with her grandmother on the family farm. TJ picks back up where she left off eight years earlier, tending to the fruit and nut tree orchard, while learning her grandmother's secret trade. Soon, TJ's high school sweetheart and the same girl who broke her heart, comes back into her life, threatening to steal it away once again. As the weeks turn into months and tragedy strikes again, TJ realizes coming home was the best thing she could've ever done.

Special Assignment by Austen Thorne. Secret Service Agent Parker Meeks has her hands full when she gets her new assignment, protecting a Congressman's teenage daughter, who has had threats made on her life and been whisked away to a Christian boarding school under an alias to finish out her senior year. Parker is fine with the assignment, until she finds out she has to go undercover as a Canon Priest. The last thing Parker expects to find is a beautiful, art history teacher, who is intrigued by her in more ways than one.

Miracle at Christmas by Sydney Canyon. A Modern Twist on the Classic Scrooge Story. Dylan is a power-hungry lawyer who pushed away everything good in her life to become the best defense attorney in the, often winning the worst cases and keeping anyone with enough money out of jail. She's visited on Christmas Eve by her deceased law partner, who threatens her with a life in hell like his own, if she doesn't change her path. During the course of the night, she is taken on a journey through her past, present, and future with three very different spirits.

Bella Vita by Sydney Canyon. Brady is the First Officer of the crew on the Bella Vita, a luxury charter yacht in the Caribbean. She enjoys the laidback island lifestyle, and is accustomed to high profile guests, but when a U.S. Senator charters the yacht as a gift to his beautiful twin daughters who have just graduated from college and a few of their friends, she literally has her hands full.

Brides (Bridal Series book 2) by Graysen Morgen. Britton Prescott is dating the love of her life, Daphne Attwood, after a few tumultuous events that happened to unravel at her sister's wedding reception, seven months earlier. She's happy with the way things are, but immense pressure from her family and friends to take the next step, nearly sends her back to the single life. The idea of a long engagement and simple wedding are thrown out the window, as both families take over, rushing Britton and Daphne to the altar in a matter of weeks.

Cypress Lake by Graysen Morgen. The small town of Cypress Lake is rocked when one murder after another happens. Dani Ricketts, the Chief Deputy for the Cypress Lake Sheriff's Office, realizes the murders are linked. She's surprised when the girl that broke her heart in high school has not only returned home, but she's also Dani's only suspect. Kristen Malone has come back to Cypress Lake to put the past behind her so that she can move on with her life. Seeing Dani Ricketts again throws her off-guard, nearly derailing her plans to finally rid herself and her family of Cypress Lake.

Crashing Waves by Graysen Morgen. After a tragic accident, Pro Surfer, Rory Eden, spends her days hiding in the surf and snowboard manufacturing company that she built from the ground up, while living her life as a shell of the person that she once was. Rory's world is turned upside down when a young surfer pursues her, asking for the one thing she can't do. Adler Troy and Dr. Cason Macauley from Graysen Morgen's bestselling novel: *Falling Snow*, make an appearance in this romantic adventure about life, love, and letting go.

Bridesmaid of Honor (Bridal Series book 1) by Graysen Morgen. Britton Prescott's best friend is getting married and she's the maid of honor. As if that isn't enough to deal with, Britton's sister announces she's getting married in the same month and her maid of honor is her best friend Daphne, the same woman who has tormented Britton for years. Britton has to suck it up and play nice, instead of scratching her eyes out, because she and Daphne are in both weddings. Everyone is counting on them to behave like adults.

Falling Snow by Graysen Morgen. Dr. Cason Macauley, a high-speed trauma surgeon from Denver meets Adler Troy, a professional snowboarder and sparks fly. The last thing Cason wants is a relationship and Adler doesn't realize what's right in front of her until it's gone, but will it be too late?

Fate vs. Destiny by Graysen Morgen. Logan Greer devotes her life to investigating plane crashes for the National Transportation Safety Board. Brooke McCabe is an investigator with the Federal Aviation Association who literally flies by the seat of her pants. When Logan gets tangled in head games with both women will she choose fate or destiny?

Just Me by Graysen Morgen. Wild child Ian Wiley has to grow up and take the reins of the hundred year old family business when tragedy strikes. Cassidy Harland is a little surprised that she came within an inch of picking up a gorgeous stranger in a bar and is shocked to find out that stranger is the new head of her company.

Love Loss Revenge by Graysen Morgen. Rian Casey is an FBI Agent working the biggest case of her career and madly in love with her girlfriend. Her world is turned upside when tragedy strikes. Heartbroken, she tries to rebuild her life. When she discovers the truth behind what really happened that awful night she decides justice isn't good enough, and vows revenge on everyone involved.

Natural Instinct by Graysen Morgen. Chandler Scott is a Marine Biologist who keeps her private life private. Corey Joslen is intrigued by Chandler from the moment she meets her. Chandler is forced to finally open her life up to Corey. It backfires in Corey's face and sends her running. Will either woman learn to trust her natural instinct?

Secluded Heart by Graysen Morgen. Chase Leery is an overworked cardiac surgeon with a group of best friends that have an opinion and a reason for everything. When she meets a new artist named Remy Sheridan at her best friend's art gallery she is captivated by the reclusive woman. When Chase finds out why Remy is so sheltered will she put her career on the line to help her or is it too difficult to love someone with a secluded heart?

In Love, at War by Graysen Morgen. Charley Hayes is in the Army Air Force and stationed at Ford Island in Pearl Harbor. She is the commanding officer of her own female-only service squadron and doing the one thing she loves most, repairing airplanes. Life is good for Charley, until the day she finds herself falling in love while fighting for her life as her country is thrown haphazardly into World War II. Can she survive being in love and at war?

Fast Pitch by Graysen Morgen. Graham Cahill is a senior in college and the catcher and captain of the softball team. Despite being an all-star pitcher, Bailey Michaels is young and arrogant. Graham and Bailey are forced to get to know each other off the field in order to learn to work together on the field. Will the extra time pay off or will it drive a nail through the team?

Submerged by Graysen Morgen. Assistant District Attorney Layne Carmichael had no idea that the sexy woman she took home from a local bar for a one night stand would turn out to be someone she would be prosecuting months later. Scooter is a Naval Officer on a submarine who changes women like she changes uniforms. When she is accused of a heinous crime she is shocked to see her latest conquest sitting across from her as the prosecuting attorney.

Vow of Solitude by Austen Thorne. Detective Jordan Denali is in a fight for her life against the ghosts from her past and a Serial Killer taunting her with his every move. She lives a life of solitude and plans to keep it that way. When Callie Marceau, a curious Medical Examiner, decides she wants in on the biggest case of her career, as well as, Jordan's life, Jordan is powerless to stop her.

Igniting Temptation by Sydney Canyon. Mackenzie Trotter is the Head of Pediatrics at the local hospital. Her life takes a rather unexpected turn when she meets a flirtatious, beautiful fire fighter. Both women soon discover it doesn't take much to ignite temptation.

One Night by Sydney Canyon. While on a business trip, Caylen Jarrett spends an amazing night with a beautiful stripper. Months later, she is shocked and confused when that same woman re-enters her life. The fact that this stranger could destroy her career doesn't bother her. C.J. is more terrified of the feelings this woman stirs in her. Could she have fallen in love in one night and not even known it?

Fine by Sydney Canyon. Collin Anderson hides behind a façade, pretending everything is fine. Her workaholic wife and best friend are both oblivious as she goes on an emotional journey, battling a potentially hereditary disease that her mother has been diagnosed with. The only person who knows what is really going on, is Collin's doctor. The same doctor, who is an acquaintance that she's always been attracted to, and who has a partner of her own.

Shadow's Eyes by Sydney Canyon. Tyler McCain is the owner of a large ranch that breeds and sells different types of horses. She isn't exactly thrilled when a Hollywood movie producer shows up wanting to film his latest movie on her property. Reegan Delsol is an up and coming actress who has everything going for her when she lands the lead role in a new film, but there one small problem that could blow the entire picture.

Light Reading: A Collection of Novellas by Sydney Canyon. Four of Sydney Canyon's novellas together in one book, including the bestsellers Shadow's Eyes and One Night.

Visit us at www.tri-pub.com

www.ingramcontent.com/pod-product-compliance
Lightning Source LLC
Chambersburg PA
CBHW031722170626
46808CB00005B/1853